Check out what RT Book Reviews *is saying about Rhonda Nelson's heroes in— and out of—uniform!*

Letters from Home
"This highly romantic tale is filled with emotion and wonderful characters. It's a heart-melting romance."

The Soldier
"Wonderfully written and heart-stirring, the story flies by to the deeply satisfying ending."

The Hell-Raiser
"A highly entertaining story that has eccentric secondary characters, hot sex and a heartwarming romance."

The Loner
"A highly romantic story with two heartwarming characters and a surprise ending."

Dear Reader,

Thank you so much for picking up *The Renegade*. I love writing about these honorable, slightly wicked heroes. They're all Southern gentlemen, so they know how to treat a lady—when they find the right one, of course—and they're all honest and noble to the core. Nothing makes a guy sexier than a sense of humor and a slow smile, and these guys always have both.

With a penchant for trouble but a knack for staying out of it, Tanner Crawford is always one step away from landing in hot water. A third-generation Ranger, Tanner has been spoon-fed a love of his country and raised to believe that words like *honor* and *duty* aren't just pretty sentiments, but a way of life. But when a mission gone wrong results in the accidental death of women and children, Tanner loses the stomach for war. That's when he finds himself working for Ranger Security and guarding Mia Hawthorne, the one girl he's never been able to forget, and a fertility statue reputed to have special powers.

Nothing brings a smile to my face faster than hearing from my readers, so be sure to check out my Web site at www.ReadRhondaNelson.com.

Happy reading!

Rhonda

Rhonda Nelson

THE RENEGADE

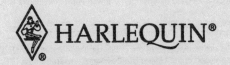

HARLEQUIN®

TORONTO • NEW YORK • LONDON
AMSTERDAM • PARIS • SYDNEY • HAMBURG
STOCKHOLM • ATHENS • TOKYO • MILAN • MADRID
PRAGUE • WARSAW • BUDAPEST • AUCKLAND

Recycling programs
for this product may
not exist in your area.

ISBN-13: 978-0-373-79561-1

THE RENEGADE

www.eHarlequin.com

Printed in U.S.A.

ABOUT THE AUTHOR

A Waldenbooks bestselling author, two-time RITA®
Award nominee and *RT Book Reviews* Reviewers'
Choice nominee, Rhonda Nelson writes hot romantic
comedy for the Harlequin Blaze line and other Harlequin
imprints. With more than twenty-five published books
to her credit and many more coming down the pike,
she's thrilled with her career and enjoys dreaming up
her characters and manipulating the worlds they live
in. In addition to a writing career she has a husband,
two adorable kids, a black Lab and a beautiful bichon
frise. She and her family make their chaotic but happy
home in a small town in northern Alabama. She loves
to hear from her readers, so be sure and check her out
at www.readRhondaNelson.com.

Books by Rhonda Nelson

HARLEQUIN BLAZE
255—THE PLAYER
277—THE SPECIALIST
283—THE MAVERICK
322—THE EX-GIRLFRIENDS' CLUB
361—FEELING THE HEAT
400—THE LONER
412—THE HELL-RAISER
475—LETTERS FROM HOME
481—THE SOLDIER
545—THE RANGER
549—BORN ON THE 4TH OF JULY "The Prodigal"

For the Poe Toaster, whoever
and wherever you are.

1

THE ONLY PENIS TANNER Crawford was accustomed to protecting was his own.

Tanner felt a disbelieving smile slide over his lips as he stared down at the picture in his hand. He could feel three sets of eyes—those of former Rangers Jamie Flanagan, Brian Payne and Guy McCann—all trained on him expectantly, waiting for his reaction. Both Jamie and Payne were poker-faced, but Guy's mouth was twitching with the effort not to laugh.

Struggling with that impulse himself, Tanner pulled in a deep breath and then looked up at the three gentleman of Ranger Security. Reminding himself that this was a new job—his first as a civilian after more than a decade at Uncle Sam's beck and call—he tried to arrange his face into something that would look professional rather than shocked and mildly revolted.

When Colonel Garrett had assured him of placement with Ranger Security, Tanner had imagined he'd be guarding glamorous socialites and the odd dignitary. Not funny little stone statues with enormous penises.

The mental adjustment took effort and he'd had enough to adjust to of late. Abrupt career change, one he'd never anticipated. Having his head shrunk repeatedly over the incident which had precipitated his quick departure from the military.

And he was still having damned nightmares.

Tanner had always been a roll-with-the-punches kind of guy, had prided himself on his ability to quickly assess and regroup, to do his job with competent enthusiasm and a level of detachment necessary to complete his mission. Dubbed "Renegade" by his fellow soldiers because of his unique ability to get the right outcome through so-called "wrong" procedures, Tanner was never truly concerned with the process so long as the end result was in his favor. War wasn't a game and loss was a natural byproduct of conflict. But no amount of heritage—he'd been a third-generation Ranger—training or detachment had prepared him for what had happened outside Mosul.

Gut-wrenching cries from mothers, wails of terror and despair from children. Broken little bodies...

It was over. Finished. Done.

Much to the displeasure of his father, who in no way supported or understood why he'd had to get out. *"Your weakness is disgraceful. Man up, son. That's Crawford blood in your veins."* Tanner smothered a bitter snort.

As if he'd ever forget.

"What is this, exactly?" he asked, pleased that his

voice sounded level. "And, more importantly, why do I need to protect it?"

Payne was the one to answer. "It's a statue of a South American fertility god. It's been on display at the Smithsonian along with various other objects of the same nature. The entire exhibit will be moving to Dallas. That's where Ranger Security—and you, specifically—come into play. You'll fly into D.C., confer with the exhibit liaison and you, the liaison and Dick here—he nodded at the picture, indicating the statue—will drive back to Dallas. For appearance's sake, a decoy will be moving with the exhibit."

Drive? But wouldn't it be more expedient to fly?

"Under ordinary circumstances, flying would be a better alternative," Payne remarked, as though reading his mind. "But this particular statue has been the target of three burglary attempts alone since it's been in D.C."

Tanner glanced down at the picture once more and gave it a dubious look. Carved out of some porous, graying stone, it was roughly a foot tall. The little man's face was crude and devoid of expression. His hands were wrapped around the root of his enormous penis, which stood away from his body in a proud, anatomically correct position. But that's where the authenticity stopped. The penis itself was taller than the statue's head. In fact, it was more penis than man. Tanner frowned.

Why in the hell would anyone want to steal this thing? Tanner wondered, genuinely puzzled. It was hideous and, for reasons he couldn't readily identify, just looking at it made him strangely uncomfortable. Though he'd always been quite pleased with his own equipment, this little relic could easily give a guy an inferiority complex.

Guy snorted and took a swallow of his energy drink. He aimed the remote control at the large flat-panel television anchored to the wall. "Hard to believe anyone would want it, isn't it?"

"Truthfully, yes." Tanner looked up, certain there had to be more to this story than he was getting. "What's the draw? What's so special about it?"

Guy chuckled and that wicked laugh left Tanner feeling distinctly uneasy. Jamie winced and looked away. Tanner's gaze shifted to Payne, who seemed more likely to supply an answer.

Payne released a small breath and, for the first time, a shadow of a smile hovered around his lips. "The draw is…it seems to work."

Tanner blinked, certain he'd misunderstood. "Come again?"

"More than seventy percent of the women who have worked directly with Dick—and roughly half of those who have merely been in close proximity to him—have become pregnant," Jamie clarified. "Those are pretty damned convincing odds."

"If you believe the hype," Guy said, his lips twisting into a doubtful smile.

Payne handed Tanner another file, this one filled with newspaper clippings and printed articles from the Internet. "The press has had a field day with it. As a result, thousands of hopeful couples have flocked to the display. And there was interest enough beforehand," he added grimly.

Tanner's antennae twitched. "Interest? From whom?"

"Private collectors," Payne said. "One, in particular. Rodrigo Ramirez. According to our research, Ramirez claims that the statue was mistakenly donated to the Smithsonian by his great-grandfather. Ernesto Ramirez was a renowned archeologist. Rodrigo is a glorified treasure hunter, whose fortune is of questionable origin. He's as unscrupulous as they come. And he's dangerous. The people who stand in his way commonly end up sporting a toe tag."

Nothing like a little danger to get the blood flowing, Tanner thought, as he studied a picture of the man in question. Designer suit, Italian shoes, porcélain veneers. The trappings were what one would expect from a wealthy businessman, but there was a cruelness around his eyes that ruined the polished effect. He could see where this man could be dangerous.

"What's kept him out of prison?" Tanner asked.

"Money mostly," Jamie said. "The charges never stick, witnesses go missing. The usual stuff."

Tanner grimaced. "Sounds like a charming guy." He looked up. "So he's the primary reason Ranger Security has been hired?"

"Yes," Payne said. "Typically the museums coordinate their own security, but given the interest and threat level directed at Dick, they decided that outsourcing the security detail on him would be the best bet."

Tanner silently agreed.

"Ramirez and the contingent of reporters following along with the so called 'fertility phenomena' won't be expecting a change in protocol, which will give you an advantage," Jamie added.

Fertility phenomena, Tanner thought. He smothered a snort. Did these people genuinely believe that this little statue—nothing more than rock—had the power to make them conceive? Were they that desperate? Evidently so, he thought, baffled.

Having had a sister who struggled with fertility issues, Tanner had an on-the-fringes look at how devastating the inability to conceive a child could be. His sister and her husband had struggled through two years of marital, financial and emotional strain before she'd finally gotten pregnant with Eli, his eighteen-month-old nephew. Would Roxanne have believed this? Tanner wondered. Would she have made the pilgrimage to see Dick if there was even a remote possibility that it might work? He sighed, knowing the answer.

Without a doubt, yes.

"Once the statue is safely in Dallas, your job is complete," Payne told him. "We don't care what route you take or how you get there, so long as the artifact and the liaison arrive safely."

Tanner nodded, knowing his dismissal was imminent. He'd been briefed on his salary—he was still reeling from the income and benefits package, though his friend Will, also of Ranger Security, had warned him, of course—and had been given the keys to his new apartment, which was right here in the building. The convenience would be a plus.

The sleek Atlanta high-rise was in a prime location in the downtown area, and had been furnished with every possible amenity. Considering Tanner had been moving from place to place for the past decade and had been in college before that, he had little in the material possessions department. Aside from his Alabama football memorabilia, of course.

Like the office and lounge—the very room he found himself in at present—the space had been decorated with an eye for electronics and comfort. Heavy leather furniture, a sleek flat-panel television and a single spectacular remote control that ran it all, including the gas-log fireplace. The kitchen had been stocked right down to the refrigerator, which included a six pack of his favorite beer and a bottle of Jameson scotch—a welcome-aboard gift from Jamie—had been on the counter. His own belongings had been shipped ahead and placed in his spare bedroom. Tanner figured he'd have time to sort through those once this initial mission was over.

Despite the fact that his new home was outfitted with every possible perk, there was something quite sterile about it. No personal photographs, no books or knick-knacks, no clutter. He'd been picking up pieces—a rug here, a painting there, a carved wooden bowl from a street vendor—for the place where he eventually settled down, but he'd never truly looked forward to putting them in place. He did now, and the realization had been a welcome surprise, a sign that he could move forward after…

Tanner shook off the thought.

In addition to the apartment, he'd been given a laptop with the interfacing technology to tap into their sophisticated system, a cell phone and a handgun along with the permit to carry concealed.

Everything had been handled flawlessly, with an eye for detail and a thoroughness that he would have expected from the legendary former Rangers.

Known as the Specialist, Brian Payne was coolly efficient and had strategy down to an art form. There was no such thing as half-assed in his world.

Jamie Flanagan purportedly sported a genius-level IQ and had been the original player until he met and married Colonel Garrett's granddaughter. With a lucky streak that bordered on the divine, Guy McCann's ability to skate the thin line between recklessness and perfection was still locker-room lore.

Tanner counted himself damned fortunate to be working with them and would have to think of some way to properly thank Colonel Garrett when time permitted. When he'd finally realized that he couldn't continue in his job—that he no longer had the stomach for war—he hadn't had any idea what he was going to do and hadn't thought far enough ahead to even consider it.

Getting out had been his only objective.

Now Phase Two of *Get Your Head Together* could commence, starting with the new job. He sincerely hoped the nightmares would end as quickly as his former career had. Even as a child, Tanner had never had nightmares. He'd never been spooked by anything that went bump in the night, could watch horror movies without batting a lash and could honestly say he'd never been truly afraid of anything.

That absence of fear had made him one helluva soldier.

But these horrific dreams absolutely terrified him.

It was the death, the helplessness, the inevitability.

The weight of knowing that he couldn't do anything at all to prevent what was happening pinned him into place, his leaden legs refused to move, to do anything that could change the dreadful outcome. And that final moment, the one that always made him sit bolt upright screaming, when the blast rocketed through the little school, tearing it and everything inside into bits and pieces, always brought him to his knees.

Tanner closed his eyes, fighting back the vision and swallowed the revulsion that automatically clawed up his throat. He fisted his hands to keep them from shaking.

"Do you have any questions?" Payne asked, his shrewd gaze missing nothing.

"The liaison," he said, determined not to screw this up. He couldn't afford to make a mistake—this was his only backup plan. There was nowhere else for him to go. Home was out of the question, of course. He'd disgraced his family. His grandfather would welcome him, but

Tanner couldn't face him right now, either. "When do I meet him?"

"You meet *her* at 8:00 a.m. tomorrow morning," Payne said. "You'll pick up a rental car at the airport, of course. Once the liaison and the statue are in your possession, you would be wise not to let either of them out of your sight."

So he wasn't just protecting the statue, he was there to protect the woman, as well. He mentally dubbed a short, plump, graying academic type in neutral colors and sensible heels into the slot of the liaison and hoped like hell she didn't have any annoying habits he'd have to deal with on the road trip. Hours upon hours trapped in the car with a denture clicker was *not* his idea of fun.

But this wasn't supposed to be fun, Tanner reminded himself. It was work. And he was damned lucky to have it.

"Her name?" he asked, consulting a file. A nanosecond later, Tanner's gaze landed on a hauntingly familiar face and shock detonated through him.

"Mia Hawthorne," Payne said, needlessly confirming what Tanner now knew. God, how long had it been? Ten years? Twelve? And yet in the space of a heartbeat and one glance at her picture, everything that had been old was new again.

Looking into those warm brown eyes, he experienced the same uncontrollable rush of desire he always had when he looked at her. Her hair was longer now, Tanner noted, which was saying something because those mink locks had been past her shoulders when they'd been in college. He distinctly remembered the feel of the strands sliding over his chest when they'd been together. The silky, heavy weight of it against the backs of his hands.

He felt Payne's gaze on him. "You know her?"

A disbelieving chuckle rumbled up Tanner's throat. "She was my Lit tutor in college," he confessed, tearing his gaze away. She was also the only girl he'd ever come remotely close to falling in love with. But he should probably keep that little nugget of insight to himself.

Jamie looked away and swore under his breath and Guy chuckled, as though this was somehow funny. Payne's expression, as usual, was unreadable. "Is this going to be a problem?" he asked.

"No," Tanner said, not quite following.

"Ha," Guy remarked. "She'll be pregnant before they get to Dallas. Did you see the look on his face? We know that look. We've seen it many times over the past several years."

Pregnant before Dallas? Who? Mia? What the fu— *Ahhhhh.* "I can assure you, she will not be pregnant before we get to Dallas," he said, infusing enough lead into his voice for all three men to take notice.

"Can you assure us you haven't slept with her before?" Guy asked.

Tanner hesitated, not willing to lie.

Guy merely smiled knowingly.

"Whether he has or hasn't isn't any of our business," Jamie said. He glared at Guy. "People who live in glass houses shouldn't cast stones, remember? Mixing business with pleasure has been a bit of a stumbling block for all of us."

Tanner knew that, too. Will had told him all about it when he'd told Tanner about his fiancée, Rhiannon. Given the successful pairings of the men who worked there, Ranger Security should go into the matchmaking business, as well, Tanner thought.

But he wasn't looking for a relationship of any sort, temporary, permanent or otherwise. He could barely stand to be in his own head at the moment, much less let anyone else inside it. He had to focus on putting his life back together, on creating a new normal. On not disappointing anyone else.

Besides, given how he and Mia had parted ways the last time they were together, he knew hooking up with her again was completely out of the question. He grimaced.

It hadn't been the right time for them back then, either.

"How do you think Ms. Hawthorne is going to react to your presence as her security detail?" Payne asked.

"She'll be shocked," he said, imagining the look on her face when he showed up as her protection. His lips twitched. "But otherwise she should be okay with it. We're both professionals, after all, with the same goal."

Protecting Dick.

Payne evaluated him for a moment longer, as though there was something else he wanted to say. Ultimately, he decided against it. He nodded once, then offered his hand. "Welcome aboard," he said.

Tanner smiled. "I'm glad to be here."

He stood and was halfway to the door before Jamie stopped him.

Tanner turned reflexively and a box whizzed its way through the air toward him. He instinctively caught it— too many years playing with a pigskin to do otherwise— then glanced down and a felt a smile roll over his lips.

Condoms.

"Just in case," Jamie said with a wink.

"THIS HAS GOT DISASTER written all over it," Guy said after their newest recruit was safely out the room. "They're former lovers." His eyes widened significantly. *"Traveling with a fertility statue."*

Though it was only 9:00 a.m. and he wasn't much of a drinker, Brian Payne pulled a Corona out of the refrigerator, popped the top and settled heavily into a leather recliner. "Did you want to go?" Payne asked Guy.

"Hell, no," he immediately replied.

"And your overall impression of Tanner?" he asked, looking at his two partners.

"Capable, but haunted," Jamie said.

Guy nodded. "And tired. Like he's not getting enough sleep."

"He's having nightmares," Jamie remarked off-handedly.

Payne arched a brow.

"He told Will and Will mentioned it to me," Jamie explained.

Having been a part of their own mission gone wrong—one in which they lost a dear friend—Payne, Jamie and Guy could certainly empathize.

War was hell.

But Will Forrester—who'd also been part of Tanner's ill-fated unit outside Mosul—was settling in nicely and had had nothing but wonderful things to say about his friend. Combined with Colonel Garrett's recommendation, hiring the former Ranger had been a no-brainer.

But the college-girl connection was a bit worrisome, particularly considering—

"Do you think we should have mentioned the other so-called side effect of being around Dick?" Guy asked, his lips twisting with familiar humor.

Payne *had* considered it and rejected the idea. Some things were better left unsaid.

Jamie chuckled and shook his head. "Tanner will figure that one out soon enough. It's a *fertility* statue, after all. And there's only one way to be fertile."

"I don't believe it," Guy said, kicking his legs out onto the coffee table in front of him. He settled more fully into the couch and snorted. "Like that little statue has the power to make you horny."

Jamie chuckled. "Sounds like Mia Hawthorne can do that well enough on her own when it comes to Tanner. Did you see the look on his face?"

Yes, he had, Payne thought speculatively. Who knew? Maybe Mia and Dick would be just the sort of distraction Tanner needed. If he was too busy thinking about having sex, maybe his dreams would take a different direction.

Payne lifted his beer. "To our newest recruit," he said.

"May he use the condoms we gave him," Jamie added.

Guy chuckled darkly, clinked his bottle against theirs. "Guess it's too much to hope that he won't need them at all."

2

"YOU SOUND LIKE A SKEPTIC, Ms. Hawthorne," the reporter remarked with a droll smile. "Do you not believe all the evidence that proves Maulu Hautu's powers are real?"

Mia pasted a smile onto her face and lied again. "I believe in the power of suggestion," she said, thankful once more when a bolt of lightning didn't rend the heavens and strike her dead. She'd never had a drama class in her life, but she was now beginning to think she'd missed her calling.

She *did* believe.

That was the problem.

Aside from the perpetual achy heaviness in her womb and the thick thread of desire constantly weaving through her blood, she'd been ridiculously preoccupied with the idea of sex since the moment she'd come into contact with Maulu Hautu.

The hot, sweaty, frantic, up-against-the-wall variety, specifically.

Considering she'd only had that sort of sex one time in her life, with a partner who had thoughtlessly set the standard then meandered on his way, Mia had been irritatingly preoccupied with the memory of *him,* as well.

Which was hardly fair to her current boyfriend who, while he didn't necessarily set her on fire, could kindle a flame that occasionally resulted in an *almost*-orgasm. Mia inwardly winced. She could feel the tingle, but never quite made it to the quake.

It was depressing as hell.

But there was a lot to be said for stability, Mia thought bracingly, for a man who wouldn't bail at the first sign of trouble. Though Harlan would never rock her world in the bedroom or make her belly flutter with a mere look, he knew how to prepare her tea and could carry on a decent conversation. Besides, there was a sardonic intellectual sexiness about him—that's what had drawn her to him in the first place. But was it enough to base a forever kind of relationship on? Mia wondered once again. She'd been asking herself that question a lot in recent weeks and, while she knew she suspected the answer, she dreaded the inevitable conversation.

Mia glanced at her watch, a silent signal to the contingent of reporters amassed in the briefing room. Almost time to go. Her security detail would be arriving soon and they would break down the exhibit, pack it up and move on to Dallas. In light of the interest in Maulu Hautu—or Moe, as she'd dubbed him—the powers that be had devised an alternate plan for transporting the increasingly popular statue, one that included her, a personal bodyguard and the little fertility god.

Admittedly the exhibit's success was a feather in her cap, but the criminal interest in Moe was definitely a fly in the ointment. She'd learned from Ed Thompson, their head of security, that they suspected a private collector by the name of Ramirez was the one behind the past three burglary attempts. As it happened, she'd met Ramirez at the opening in Atlanta and, though she'd noticed the affected air of wealth around the older man, there was something chilling—strangely reptilian and knowing—in his eyes. She'd felt dirty after shaking his hand and had made a point to avoid him when he'd shown up here in Washington, too.

"Are you anticipating a large crowd in Dallas?" Freddie Ackerman, the eccentric, tenacious reporter who had dogged the exhibit's every move for the past several weeks, asked. He'd recently started traveling with a round-faced assistant who seemed to be under the deluded impression that her boss hung the moon. It was sad proof that there was a nut for every screw, even if hers hadn't made an appearance yet.

Freddie had been waiting for his big break and, for reasons Mia couldn't begin to fathom, he'd decided Maulu Hautu was it. Since she was the mobile curator for the exhibit—which had been *her* big break—Freddie had been shadowing her every move.

This new plan was sure to thwart him, she thought with a private grin while framing a reply.

"We are, Mr. Ackerman." She smiled. "Due to the

media's interest in Fertility Through The Ages—" the crowd tittered as she purposely put her tongue in cheek "—we're expecting record turnouts in Dallas."

Freddie's gaze sharpened. "Can you tell us, have there been any additional burglary attempts?"

"No," she said, lying smoothly once again. In fact, there had been one last night. The guy had been an amateur, though, and he'd been easily deflected. The attempt, nevertheless, rattled her cage. Mia released a small breath.

Nothing would make her happier than getting on the road—away from the scrutiny, in particular—with the security expert. She could hand over the reins to him for a while—inasmuch as she was able—and simply relax. She'd filled her iPod with old Monty Python movies, lots of show tunes and had packed her knitting needles and enough yarn to circle the globe. She was actually looking forward to the drive, to watching beloved movies and knitting her way from D.C. to Dallas, to letting the passing landscape and road noise soothe her frayed nerves. Though this plan hadn't been her idea, she wholeheartedly approved of it.

Speaking of which, it was time to get moving. "I'm afraid that's all the time there is, ladies and gentlemen." Her gaze slid to Ackerman and his cohort. She felt her lips twitch. "I'm sure I'll see some of you in Dallas."

Grizzled and gray with Newman blue eyes, an unfortunate sense of style and a small port wine stain on his cheek, Ackerman merely smiled at her and inclined his head.

No doubt he'd booked a seat on her flight, Mia thought. Pity for him she wouldn't be on the plane. She felt a twinge of regret on his behalf for that. Something about the old guy tugged at her heartstrings. Even though he was surly and obnoxious with a bulldog reputation for always finding the facts, he reminded her of her grandfather. All bark and no bite. She'd lost him years ago, but remembered him fondly. Ackerman, for whatever reason, stirred the same sentiment.

Briskly descending the stairs down the platform in her customary heels, Mia clicked her way through the little throng of people and exited the room. Sophie, her own assistant, was waiting on her. Bright-eyed, brilliant and clumsy to the point that she was almost disabled, Sophie wore a huge smile and excitement pulsed around her in waves. Her platinum curls ringed her head in a halo of light. She put Mia in mind of an absurdly happy puppy, waiting for a bone.

"He's here," she said significantly, the words practically bursting out of her.

"Who? Oh, the gentleman from Ranger Security?" Mia said, as understanding dawned. Excellent. He was punctual. She appreciated timeliness. While being late was occasionally unavoidable, a habitual offender signaled a disrespectful lack of regard for other people's time. Frankly, it pissed her off to no end.

Her mother, God rest her soul, had never managed to make it anywhere on time, including her own funeral, Mia thought with a wry smile. The hearse had picked up a nail, resulting in a flat tire on the way to the cemetery.

Though the funeral director had been properly horrified and apologetic, the sheer predictability of her mother's ability to be late—even in death—had loosened the choke hold of grief Mia had been trying to claw away from her neck. The humor of the situation had enabled her to laugh while she was grieving. That had been three years ago and there wasn't a day that went by when she didn't think of her, Mia thought.

She never spared a thought for her father, though. The faithless bastard didn't deserve it. The last time she'd seen him had been at the funeral. His appearance had been an unwelcome surprise on more than one level. He'd been unshaven, dirty and knee-walking drunk. And the pièce de résistance? He'd needed a "loan." He'd been trying to contact her over the past few weeks and had left messages with Harlan, but Mia hadn't returned his calls and never planned to. As far as she was concerned, she'd become an orphan when her mother died.

Honestly, how her mother had ever gotten involved with Charlie Hawthorne was beyond Mia's scope of understanding. She'd asked her mother once, years after he'd left. Her mother had merely shrugged and told her love was blind. In that case it would have had to have been deaf and dumb, too. It boggled the mind. Charlie was handsome enough she supposed—dark hair, dark eyes—and she imagined to her mother, who'd been raised by strict Irish Catholic parents, he was the forbidden bad boy.

He was bad, all right.

Though he'd never been physically abusive to her

mother, Mia remembered her father as an unconcerned selfish man more interested in boozing it up with his friends and televised sports than his wife or child. He'd been a thug, a petty criminal determined to avoid legitimate work. She did have one nice memory of him though, one that she dragged out on the occasions when she was feeling particularly bitter.

It had been the summer she'd turned five. She'd learned to ride the neighbor's bike and had desperately wanted one of her own. Her mother had told her that if she was a good girl, Santa might see fit to get her a new bike for Christmas. But to Mia Christmas was too late.

Her father had agreed and had gone down to the hardware store and bought her a brand-new hot pink-and-white bike with gleaming hot pink streamers and a dazzling white wicker hand basket with flowers on the front. She'd woken up to see it sitting at the foot of her bed the next morning. She'd been overjoyed, ecstatic and absolutely over the moon. She remembered hugging her father, delighted by his unusual generosity, and being mildly resentful of her mother, who had wanted to wait on Santa Claus.

What she hadn't known until much later was that her father had stolen the money from her mother's purse—the cash she'd tucked back to pay the electricity bill—and her mother had ultimately had to pawn a ring that had been given to her by her grandmother to cover the bill. Mia had a picture of that ring—a large opal surrounded by a band of small diamonds and trimmed with baguette rubies—and was still combing pawnshops, antiques malls and online auctions, hoping she might be able to recover it. Fruitless probably, but she'd always felt horribly guilty about it. She hadn't been directly responsible, of course, but that didn't change the way she felt.

Closing the door on that line of thinking, Mia straightened her shoulders, looked at Sophie and quirked a brow. "First impression?"

"Gorgeous," Sophie said instantly with a dreamy smile.

Mia chuckled. "While interesting, that's not what I meant. Does he look capable?"

"He looks like a badass," her assistant said, practically shivering all over. "Like he could break you into small pieces and make you think it was your idea."

Had she mentioned Sophie had a flair for the dramatic, as well? Mia smiled wryly. "He sounds quite interesting."

Actually, he didn't sound anything at all like the retired police officer she'd been imagining as her security guard. For whatever reason, she'd had a brawnier Columbo in mind.

"He's got great eyes," Sophie told her as they made their way down the hall. "They're the palest green I've ever seen and ringed in dark blue." She released an unsteady breath. "It's quite…arresting."

She'd seen a pair of eyes like before, Mia thought with a jolt of shock. They belonged to the same guy she'd been fantasizing about with increasing frequency over the past several weeks. Unbidden, a tingle of unease slid up her spine. Ridiculous, she thought, shaking the sensation off. It was impossible. The odds of Tanner Crawford being her security detail were greater than the odds of her becoming the next Miss America.

Slim to none.

After all, to start on the pageant tour, she'd need to lose twenty pounds, grow five inches and get breast implants, none of which she was willing or able to do. But that was okay. She was comfortable in her own skin, liked her rather curvy body and had invested in good makeup and good foundation garments to accentuate the positive.

"And his lips," Sophie continued, seemingly determined to list this man's every attribute. "Wide, full and sculpted, like they should belong on a Greek statue. Very Romanesque," she said, punctuating the statement with another dreamy sigh. She turned a hopeful face in Mia's direction. "Are you sure you don't need me to go with you? I *am* your personal assistant, after all."

"I'm sure," Mia replied with a chuckle. "I need you to travel with the exhibit. You're my eyes and ears on the scene."

Sophie's face fell. "But—"

Mia tucked a wayward strand of hair behind her ear. "Where is he?"

"He's waiting for you in the lounge," her assistant said glumly.

"Excellent. I'm thirsty."

Because her mouth had gone inexplicably dry and her

palms had begun to sweat. Sophie's further description of her new security guard was sounding more and more like the guy she'd been thinking about, the blast from her past, former football player turned ROTC soldier, Tanner Crawford. Last she heard he was a Ranger—the thought made her smile because she knew that had been his dream—serving in Iraq.

More bookworm than beauty queen, Mia had been Tanner's English tutor when they'd attended the University of Alabama together. On the surface Tanner had been the quintessential jock, handsome, cocky and above all, popular. Like many other girls roaming the campus who'd been dazzled by his easy athletic grace and effortless appeal, Mia had been just as charmed from afar.

When her professor had approached her about the tutoring opportunity, she'd accepted without even inquiring about the student because she'd needed the money. Her scholarship fund only went so far and her mother needed to bank every penny she could into retirement.

So it had come as a great shock when Tanner Crawford had walked into the room, awaiting his introduction. Though his trademark irreverence and confidence were in place, it was the merest hint of reserve—that honest but unexpected shyness—she'd caught in those amazing eyes that had ultimately drawn her in. In that instant, she, a lowly campus nobody, had been able to identify with the notorious football star.

And that had been the end of her, of course.

Or of her heart and virginity, at the very least.

There had been much more behind that handsome face than she'd ever expected. She'd discovered a keen mind more interested in American and English Literature than Classical, with a fondness for Edgar Allan Poe. She'd also learned that he had a brave and noble heart, one that had given up a prime football scholarship in favor of the ROTC program and a sense of honor and integrity that was almost nostalgic. Tanner Crawford was one of those rare guys who'd actually known what he wanted to do with the rest of his life, who'd been thinking past the next game, past the next keg party, past the end of his dick.

He'd wanted to be a Ranger—just like his father and grandfather—and that surety of purpose, that maturity had been particularly attractive.

The only problem with a guy that focused was that there wasn't room for anything else in his life, including a permanent significant other. Giving her the galling and equally dreaded it's-not-you-it's-me-let's-be-friends speech shouldn't have come as a shock…but it had.

She'd been heartbroken and mortified.

While she'd been thinking about monogrammed hand towels and sharing a king-size bed till-death-do-us-part, Tanner had been trying to find a delicate way to cut her loose.

Having grown up without a father, without the traditional home, Mia had wanted the picture-perfect life. The white fence, barbecues in the backyard, a three-bedroom two-bath brick house in a trendy subdivision, where she could plant flowers and grow her own herbs.

They'd lived in shabby rentals until her senior year of high school, when her mother had been able to take the money she'd been saving for college and put it toward a home because Mia had landed a full scholarship to the university. It had been wonderful to ease that burden for her mom, who'd never had a fallback plan, who'd always been the first line of defense between them and poverty. Her grandfather helped when he could, but most of his savings had been eaten up by hospital bills for her grandmother, who'd suffered with multiple strokes until her death.

Mia had admired her mother, but had wanted a different life.

One with Tanner.

Because she would have rather died than let him know how he'd hurt her, Mia had pasted a smile onto her face and pretended that she agreed, that things had gotten too serious too soon. Then, even though she'd saved her virginity until she could be with someone she loved—Tanner—she'd promptly gone out and slept with the first guy who showed the barest hint of interest. She wasn't proud of it now and wished she could get a do-over for that night, but at the time, it was the only thing she could think of to do that might make her feel better. As much as she'd needed to overwrite the memory of him, she'd needed to feel desirable even more.

Neither goal had been achieved and she'd never shown herself the same sort of disrespect again.

She'd also gotten her one and only tattoo to mark the occasion, but she didn't regret that. The Bard's "What's past is prologue" was stamped in black ink in elaborate script across the small of her back.

Live and learn, Mia thought now as she pushed through the break-room doors. Without the benefit of mistakes, life's lessons would have a lot less impact.

And speaking of impact…

Despite her premonition, she was not prepared.

Tanner Crawford stood in the middle of the room with Ed Thompson, head of security. His gaze immediately tangled with hers and not the least bit of surprise flickered in those pale green eyes, indicating he'd known of her involvement.

A heads-up would have been nice, Mia thought, fighting the involuntary urge to smile at him. He'd broken her heart. She shouldn't want to smile at him and yet, despite the suddenly queasy feeling in her belly, she couldn't deny the absolute delight she felt upon seeing him again. The reaction was every bit as physical as the instant rush of desire winding through her limbs, the tingle of sexual awareness that ignited in her nipples within mere seconds of laying eyes on him. She suddenly felt plugged in, turned on and ready for immediate action. The fine hairs on her arms stood on end and the tips of her fingers and toes suddenly prickled with sensation.

Lust, quite inconveniently, hit her with a vengeance.

It was too much to hope for that he would have put on a few pounds and lost a considerable amount of his hair, Mia thought, her gaze skimming over a body that was bigger and harder than it had been in college. She released a shallow breath.

Badass, indeed.

He wore a pair of pleated khaki pants, which emphasized a narrow waist, and a black Henley T-shirt. The fabric stretched across his perfectly sculpted torso and hugged the broad planes of his shoulders. His arms, works of art in and of themselves, were corded with vein and muscle and dusted with a fine layer of tawny golden hair. A peek of tattoo rested just below the hem of his shirt, making her immediately curious as to what it was and why he'd gotten it. He rested on the balls of his feet, rangy, still and ready for action.

Time had been every bit as busy on his face as it had the rest of his body. Though the general topography was the same, maturity had chiseled away the youthful boyishness that used to round out the edges, leaving his jaw more angular, his cheeks hollow and the sleek slope of his brow more severe. His mouth was every bit as full and purely sinful as it had always been and the smile that kicked up the corner of his lips was at once familiar and different.

What hadn't changed were his eyes.

That unique shade, the almond shape, the faint laugh lines at the corners. That had been one of her favorite places to kiss, Mia remembered now. She let go an imperceptible breath as longing suddenly knifed through her.

Though neither her smile nor step faltered, belated panic suddenly hit her. Her, him and Moe trapped together for a minimum of twenty-one hours in a car, divided up into what could conceivably be four to five days. *Holy hell*.

She felt her smile turn painful.

Tanner Crawford was her sexual kryptonite, the last cookie on the plate, the only guy who'd *ever* rung her bell or made her sing the hallelujah chorus. He was the only lover she'd had who'd ever given her an orgasm without any "outside" help, as it were. He had what she'd jokingly dubbed The Magical Penis because it was the only one that had ever truly worked for her.

Meanwhile, thanks to Moe, she as suffering from a chronic case of Ineedtogetlaid*now*.

This was a disaster of epic proportions, Mia thought as Tanner bent forward and brushed a kiss against her cheek. Pleasure arced through her. He was like one giant self-destruct button and she wanted to press herself against him to set it off. Not good. A hot shiver surged through her and settled warmly in her sex. She bit her lip against the sensation and savored the scent of him. Something warm and musky with a cool finish. Mouthwatering.

"Mia, it's been a long time," he said, his voice the same husky baritone she remembered, a bit deeper maybe. Like a good whiskey, it had only gotten better with age.

God help her.

3

BECAUSE HE'D PREPARED himself for the tsunami-like wave of lust he knew would hit him when he saw Mia again, Tanner was ready. He'd put his game face on, had indulged in a little self-gratification last night to take the edge off and was as mentally focused as he could possibly be.

What was completely unexpected and therefore unplanned for was the wallop of sheer emotion—a disconcerting combination of joy, relief and desperation—that had him suddenly wondering if his testosterone levels were low. Men weren't supposed to feel like this, dammit. These were chick feelings and he didn't like them one bleeding bit. He determinedly bent forward and brushed a kiss against her cheek, vaguely noting that she smelled like peaches, and felt her ripe breasts press against his chest.

Predictably he went hard and those jarring softer emotions thankfully retreated as swiftly as they'd arrived.

"Mia, it's been a long time," he murmured, surprised when his voice stayed even. He felt like he was flying apart on the inside, had that same breathless-in-the-gut feeling he always got when taking a jump. Insane, he thought. She was just a girl, could have possibly been *the* girl, but still, was just a girl all the same.

She made a curious little choked sound in her throat and drew back. "It has. How have you been?"

Ed arched an interested brow. "You two know each other?"

"We do," Mia confirmed with a single nod. "We, er... We went to college together."

And had wild, down-and-dirty sex on a table in the library, Tanner added silently. *And beneath the table. And against the wall.* He watched her pulse flutter wildly in her throat, her cheeks pinken and knew that he wasn't the only one taking a fond stroll down Great Sex Memory Lane.

Ed inclined his dark head. "Well that should make this easier then, eh? A long trek like this will be much better with someone you know instead of a total stranger. I'm sure you'll have plenty to talk about. Do some catching up."

Mia's smile wavered and she darted him a quick look at Tanner. "Oh, definitely," she said, lying with more skill than he remembered. He filed that away for future consideration, then gave her a little grin to let her know he'd picked up on it.

Time to get rid of Ed, Tanner thought. He turned to the older gentleman, stuck out his hand and slapped the man on the back with friendly camaraderie. "Ed, thanks for bringing me up to speed. We'll be in contact."

"I'm sure both the statue and Mia will be in good hands," Ed said, nodding thoughtfully.

Mia made another little strangling noise, then cleared her throat. "G-got a tickle," she said, putting a finger against her neck. She started toward the vending machine. "I just need to get a drink."

Slightly bemused at her odd behavior, Tanner merely stood back and observed. She chose a bottled water from the machine and seemed to purposely keep her back to him while she took a swallow. After a minute, she took a deep breath, then exhaled and turned around to face him. Evidently once more in default mode, she'd engaged the reset button and was seemingly ready to deal with him again. Interesting. Also gratifying. He liked that he'd rattled her.

Warm brown eyes, set in a classical heart-shaped face, regarded him with equal parts curiosity and reservation and a small smile tugged at the corners of her full, unbelievably carnal mouth. Her dark hair spilled over her shoulders and down to the middle of her back, with a single large curl resting invitingly around the swell of her breast. She wore a white silk scoop-necked top beneath a fitted purple jacket and matching skirt. She had a true Renaissance figure, Tanner noted, with a small waist and lush curves—which had grown even more sensually rounded with age—and a pair of frighteningly high, incredibly sexy black heels.

He looked pointedly at the over-the-top heels and

raised a brow. "Regular footwear not dangerous enough for you?"

She kicked her foot out and twisted her ankle to admire her shoes. "It's one way to live on the edge."

When had she ever wanted to live on the edge? Tanner wondered. Last he remembered, she wanted a dependable husband, a mortgage and a minivan. The ultimate American Dream, à la Normal Rockwell and '50s sitcoms. He grimaced.

His dreams had been decidedly different, which was no small part of the reason they'd broken up.

"They can't be comfortable," he told her, skeptically eying the sliver of pointy heel. He mentally stripped her of every ounce of clothing save the shoes, and the image was so hot it could have burned his retinas.

Mia looked at him as though he were pityingly clueless. "Shoes like these aren't meant to be comfortable. They're meant to be admired and appreciated. They're jewelry for the feet."

"Foot jewelry? Seriously?"

She smirked and shook her head. "What sort of gun is that under your jacket?"

"It's a Glock 21 .45ACP with octogonal bore, single-position feed, staggered column type, thirteen rounds," he rattled off without thinking.

Her lips twisted. "Bibbidi bobbidi boo," she said. "I didn't understand a single thing beyond Glock."

He chuckled and shook his head. "You're comparing my gun to your shoes?"

"In a manner of speaking."

"But my gun is practical and your shoes are...not."

"Ah, but your gun wouldn't be practical to me," she said, lifting her shoulders in a small shrug. "It's all relative."

"I can defend myself with my gun," he added.

Her lips twitched. "One would hope. Otherwise, you'd be a sorry excuse for a security agent."

Tanner laughed again, reminded of her somewhat skewed sense of humor. It was smart, offbeat and occasionally biting, but admirable all the same. He'd missed that about her, too, he realized. He'd missed that jagged, tongue-in-cheek wit. "Too true," he told her.

"So what have you been up to?" she asked. "No longer in the military, I assume."

He felt his skin tighten around his eyes and his gut clench. "That's right. Less than a month, in fact."

"So you're new to the security business?"

"New but capable," he told her, lest she think his inexperience was going to be a problem. He'd been protecting his country, disarming terrorists and fighting insurgents, dammit. He was fully capable of moving a little statue from Point A to Point B without a problem. He'd already outlined a plan and scouted ahead to avoid road construction and heavier traffic.

Her gaze sharpened and he belatedly remembered how easily she'd always been able to read him, as though by simply cocking her head or narrowing her eyes, she could fine-tune the reception and pick the thoughts right out of his brain. It was as galling and unnerving as it had always been and he made a mental note to be more careful.

"Needed a change of scenery, eh?" she asked, unerringly going straight to the heart of the matter. The grisly images taunted him once more and he gave a dry bark of laughter.

"In a manner of speaking," he said, throwing her words back at her. He straightened. "So are you ready to go? Do we need to drop by your place and pick anything up?"

She winced. "My place is in Savannah, so that would be a little difficult. But I do need to change clothes and pick up my stuff."

"Savannah?" he asked, startled. He'd just assumed that she was in D.C., that her work with the museum kept her here.

"Yes. I've been there for several years now."

"You don't work for the Smithsonian Institute?" Dammit, he should have checked up on her, looked her up on Google at the very least, but he'd convinced himself that it wasn't necessary. That, ultimately, it didn't matter. She was just part of a job and poking into her past would somehow weaken his ability to keep that in perspective. He'd concentrated his efforts on Ramirez and Ackerman, a zealous reporter who gave him pause, and all the other people connected with the exhibit. He'd purposely avoided looking into her background because he'd been too damned curious about her and couldn't distinguish if his interest was personal or professional.

Clearly that had been a mistake, one that he deeply regretted now because it made him look foolish.

She shook her head, obviously surprised that he didn't know that already. "Not directly, no. I work for the Southern Center of Antiquities, which is based in Savannah. We're privately funded so we've got a little more authority over our interests. My director, in particular, is interested in South American culture. I did postgraduate studies in Brazil, so naturally, I was eager to participate in this exhibit. It's my big break of sorts. My first as a liaison, in fact."

She didn't precisely preen, but it was obvious that she was quite proud of herself. Her first job as a liaison, his first assignment for Ranger Security. There was a lot more than Dick's safety riding on this, Tanner suddenly realized.

Neither one of them could afford for him to make a mistake. And he'd already made his first by not investigating her further.

Shit.

"So you've been living in a hotel for the past several weeks?"

"With my boyfriend, actually," she corrected. "He's got a place here."

He felt her revelation reverberate through him and, though it was incredibly irrational, he was suddenly humiliatingly jealous of the faceless, nameless man. Was there no end to his own stupidity?

Determined not to look like an idiot or say anything dim-witted, Tanner merely inclined his head. "Ah. Does he know you're going to be traveling with me?" Great. He'd failed, once again. That question sounded entirely too self-important, and he immediately regretted it.

"Not with you specifically, but he knows that I will be accompanying the statue with the security agent." Her gaze turned speculative, as though she were considering something, but then her brow smoothed and she straightened briskly. "I suppose we should get on the road. I'm assuming you've plotted our route?"

His lips twisted. Still bossy, he saw. As if he'd show up without a plan. As if he didn't know how to read a map. As if he hadn't already made reservations at pre-selected hotels and viewed their layouts to accommodate the swiftest exit plan. Sheesh. What did she take him for? Then again, he wasn't off to a great start. "Nah," he told her, shoving his hands into his pockets. "I thought I'd drive around aimlessly for a little while."

She blinked, startled. "To throw off any would-be pursuers?"

He gave his head a small shake, pushed open the door and waited for her to pass. "That would be my secondary objective."

"What's the first?"

"To irritate the hell out of you. Of course, I've planned our route," he said, exasperated.

To his surprise, she actually laughed, a soft husky sound that made something hot slither around his middle and squeeze. "That's a mission I'm absolutely certain you'll accomplish. With little to no effort," she added.

He grinned. "I'm that good, eh, Bossy?"

She rolled her eyes and a little furrow emerged between her fine, arched brows. "Nobody's called me that in years."

"And yet the seemingly uncontrollable urge to direct is still evident," he drawled, opening her car door before she could do it herself. "Your minions are either too respectful or too terrified to comment on it." He winked at her. "I'll let you know what conclusion I come to later."

"I'll be waiting with bated breath."

Tanner chuckled and a small part of the tension he'd been carrying around for months slid off his shoulders.

One thing was for certain, this mission damned sure wasn't going to be boring, not with Mia and Dick around.

"I DON'T THINK MIA IS traveling with the exhibit this time."

The man paused to consider what his informant had just said and his eyes narrowed. "Why is that?"

"Because she left the museum with a man I've never seen before."

"Couldn't it have been her boyfriend?"

There was a snort. "This guy didn't look like any professor I've ever seen. He was fit, cagey. Put me in mind of a cop, actually."

Well, that changed things then, didn't it? Honestly, this was beginning to get tiresome. He just wanted the statue. He'd stolen dozens of other things—more valuable and better guarded—than this and those items hadn't been anywhere near as much trouble. That's what happened when you outsourced, the man thought. Quality control became a real bitch. Of course, he had other reasons for putting a lackey in place.

"Follow her to the airport," he instructed.

"And if she doesn't go to the airport?"

"Then pull something out of your bag of tricks and follow her wherever she goes. She's headed to Dallas, ultimately. I can't imagine why she would suddenly stop moving with her staff, but if that's the case, then there's a reason." A significant one, he imagined. He paused, continued to sort through possibilities. "And let me know if this guy goes with her. That could be important."

"Certainly."

It would be interesting to see what Mia did. He couldn't imagine the thorough little liaison would abandon Maula Hautu in light of the attempted thefts. Even though it wasn't her job to provide security, she was ultimately responsible for the entire exhibit. In short, it was her ass on the line if things went wrong. That's why he'd been watching her, monitoring what *she* did.

She was a key player in a game she didn't know she was playing and wasn't equipped to handle. And he had no qualms about taking her out if she stood in his way.

IT FELT EXTREMELY WEIRD to see Tanner inside Harlan's apartment. He was too big, too masculine, too…*much* for the sedate space she'd come to associate with her calm, intellectual boyfriend. Harlan preferred earth tones, natural woods and was a firm believer in right angles. No caddy-cornering things here, she thought, although she silently admitted she'd occasionally adjust a stack of magazines, the coasters or the magnets on the refrigerator just to irritate him. The passive-aggressive rebellion never failed to give her a wicked little thrill. She winced.

She realized she was in a sorry damned state when *that's* what qualified as both wicked and thrilling in her book.

Her nerves already frayed and stretched to the breaking point—after only a mere thirty minutes in Tanner's company—Mia hurriedly changed clothes, then gathered up Moe and dragged her rolling suitcase and toiletry bag into the living room.

Tanner was scanning pictures and books crammed into the shelves on either side of the fireplace. *"The Count of Monte Cristo,"* he said, sliding a finger down the spine. "It's always been a favorite of mine. Lord Byron," he said, inclining his head. "A favorite of yours, if memory serves. *Don Juan,* specifically, right?"

She nodded, too surprised to speak.

He pulled out of volume of Shakespeare. *"The Taming of the Shrew,* also a favorite I seem to recall." He tsked under his breath and shot her a reproachful look. "But no Poe, I see."

Tanner had always loved Edgar Allan Poe, and had been a huge fan of *The Raven* and *Annabelle Lee* in particular. She remembered discussing the troubled author

with him at length, arguing over his genius and character. Mia would admit that the guy had been a genius, but
the fact that he'd married his thirteen-year-old cousin
when he'd been twenty-six was a bit of a sticking point
with her. It didn't discount the work, she knew, but it
had always colored her opinion of it.

Tanner snagged her attention by gesturing to a picture of her and Harlan that had been taken on a Carib-
bean cruise the previous summer. She wore a yellow
sundress and big floppy hat. Having suffered from sun
poisoning as a child, Harlan's svelte frame was dressed
in long-sleeves and pants, and his face was covered in
thick white sunblock. He'd looked like an albino scare-
crow, she thought, wincing at the uncharitable thought.
If he'd had his way, they'd have been vacationing in
cooler climes, but he'd indulged her because she'd always loved the sun.

"St. Lucia?" Tanner asked.

"Cozumel," she corrected.

"The water's amazing, isn't it? The prettiest, clearest
blue I've ever seen."

She was surprised. She'd never imagined Tanner
would take that sort of vacation while in the military.
"You've been to Cozumel?"

"After graduation," he said, shooting her an awkward
smile. "Before I officially began my military career."

No doubt the entire football team and the cheerlead-
ing squad—hell, probably the majorettes, as well—had
gone on that trip, Mia thought, a sour taste developing

on her tongue. She turned a stack of coasters and tried to loosen her jaw. "I guess you've traveled a pretty good bit."

Something in her voice must have betrayed her because he regarded her steadily for a moment before answering. "Mostly to war zones and third-world countries, though I have managed to spend a little time in better places. Germany was surprising. All those castles." He leafed through another book, then returned it to its place. "Prague is one of the most beautiful cities I've ever seen. London, Paris, Rome, of course. I hated Paris, but the beauty of the French countryside offered redemption. Rolling hills and vineyards, stone fences and cottages. Very bucolic and picturesque."

"Have you ever thought about going back?"

"You mean, live there permanently?" he asked, as though the idea had never occurred to him. "No," he admitted. "I've got a touch of wanderlust—I love seeing other places, drinking in the culture, colors and landscape—but I'm a country boy at heart." He flashed her an authentic aw-shucks grin. "Nothing will ever be lovelier than those Carolina hills."

"So you're back in Asheville?"

His face froze and a shadow moved behind his gaze. "No, I'm in Atlanta."

"That's right," she said. "That's where Ranger Security is based. I'd forgotten."

A long dimple appeared in his left cheek and those pale green eyes crinkled in the corners. "Checked them out, did you?"

Mia blushed, but stubbornly lifted her chin. "You bet your ass I did. After all, if something goes wrong, it's my *ass* on the line here." She patted the nondescript backpack that housed the valuable statue. "If anything happens to Moe. I'm the one who will be unemployable."

He frowned. "Moe?"

"My nickname for him," she explained. She pushed her hair away from her face. "Maulu Hautu is a bit of a mouthful."

Tanner grinned, poked his tongue in his cheek and shrugged lazily. The gesture was so inherently sexy, it should been against the law. "We've just been calling him Dick."

She flattened her lips to keep them from twitching, then bit the inside of her cheek for good measure. "For obvious reasons, I prefer Moe."

"We're Southern, you know," he said, rocking back on his heels. "We could always go with a double name. Sort of like Brenda Sue and Erma Jean." His eyes twinkled. "Moe Dick."

She had to bite her lip, but could feel the smile slipping from beneath her teeth. "I don't think so."

"You gotta admit, it's got a ring to it. Moe Dick." He nodded once. "I like it."

She rolled her eyes. "Only because it's lewd."

"Which makes it all the more appropriate."

Since she couldn't argue with that, Mia simply shook her head. "I'm going to call him Moe. You can call him whatever you want to."

"I would have anyway," he said, as if she needed that reminder. Tanner had always done things his way. Ridiculously, it was part of his appeal. He nodded briskly, then looked down at the bags at her feet. "Is this everything?"

She nodded, suddenly nervous. "My laptop and camera are in the attaché case in the car."

He blew out a breath, took the backpack from her shoulders and draped it across his own. Moe had been placed in a foam-lined locking metal box to insure his safe passage.

Apprehension worked its way across her brow. "I could have—"

He opened the door for her—more of that courtesy she'd remembered about him—then easily hefted her luggage and followed her down the sidewalk. "Though I know this goes against everything in that tightly wound, autocratic only-I-can-do-it-right little body of yours, Mia, you're going to have to let me do my job."

She knew he was right, yet couldn't resist arguing with him. "Just because I have more confidence in my own ability than of others doesn't make me tightly wound or autocratic." She resisted the urge to point out to him that the luggage had wheels, that he didn't have to carry it. Idiot. No doubt the wheels impugned his masculinity.

"And yet you are both." He gave his head a mystified shake. "Go figure."

She locked the door to Harlan's apartment and flipped the dead bolt. "Smart-ass."

She started down the walk and ran headlong into the back of him. "Umph. What are you—"

"We've got company," he murmured quietly.

Panic punched her heart into a quicker rhythm. "What? Who?" She peered around an impressive biceps and swore under her breath. "That's—"

"Freddie Ackerman. *Miami Herald,*" he finished in a cool all-business voice, and she couldn't help but be impressed. Though she would have expected nothing less, it was clear Tanner had done his homework—on everything but her. No doubt they wouldn't agree on his technique, but she knew he was fully capable of taking care of both her and Moe. "I understand he's been following the exhibit for weeks now. Got a bit of a bulldog reputation, on the fringes of being unscrupulous."

"Yes," she confirmed. Tanner resumed his pace. "What's he doing here?" she whispered frantically. "He should be on his way to the airport." Actually, he should already be at the airport, making his way through those hellish security lines. She couldn't imagine why he was here, or how he'd found her. It was beyond odd.

"I'll handle it," Tanner told her. "You play along."

A red flag instantly went up. Play along? She didn't like the sound of that at all. It put him in charge and her at his mercy.

For reasons she couldn't begin to explain she had the oddest feeling that that the next few days of her life were going to be precisely like that.

Him in charge, her at his mercy.

To her consternation, a wicked thrill swirled in her

belly. She didn't know what was more disconcerting—
that she was going to be with him for the next several
days.

Or that she was going to like it.

4

WEARING A WRINKLED suit and a smug smile, Ackerman turned to them as they made their way down the walkway. "Ms. Hawthorne," he said, his gaze glancing off Tanner and landing directly on Mia. "You won't mind if I follow you to the airport, will you?"

"Whether she does or she doesn't is irrelevant," Tanner told the short, stocky man. "*I mind*. Who the hell are you?"

If there was one thing in the world he hated, it was a damned bully. And Freddie Ackerman, while not the biggest one he'd ever seen, had enough of the traits to seriously piss Tanner off. The old reporter had been so intent on trying to rattle Mia, he'd completely dismissed *Tanner* as a threat.

Big mistake.

Seemingly startled, Ackerman glanced up at him. Tanner watched the shorter man reassess, then make his second mistake—he underestimated him.

"Freddie Ackerman," he said. "*Miami Herald*. I've

been following the Maulu Hautu phenomenon and Ms. Hawthorne has been quite helpful."

"So helpful that you think it's okay to show up at her place of residence and tell her you're going to follow her?" Tanner narrowed his eyes. "Sounds a bit like stalking to me."

"And just who are you?" Freddie asked in a patronizing tone that instantly put Tanner's teeth on edge.

Tanner took a menacing step forward, purposely making the shorter man look up and step back. He adjusted his voice so that it came out low and lethal and was gratified when he saw the first hint of fear widen the man's gaze. "I'm the kind of guy who doesn't like it when other men try to follow my girlfriend, that's who I am." He looked over his shoulder at her. "Baby, has this guy been bothering you? You want me to take care of him?"

Mia's eyes were round and startled, but she collected herself enough to play along. "Honey, you know I hate picking people's teeth out of your knuckles. Besides, a trip to jail would ruin our plans." She reached forward and rubbed his arm. "You can let Mr. Ackerman go." She looked pointedly at Freddie. "I'll see you in Dallas, Freddie," she said, and made a little shooing gesture, as though he should go while she still had control over her Neanderthal of a boyfriend. "You'd better go on before you miss your flight."

"Shouldn't you be going, as well?"

Losing patience and growing more irritated by the minute, Tanner took another step forward. Sheesh, what was up with this guy? Why was he so interested in where Mia was going? "It's none of your damned business where she's going or how she gets there," he said. "In fact, it seems damned odd to me that you're so interested in her."

"Not in her," Ackerman said, genuine surprise widening his eyes. "In the exhibit."

"The exhibit will be in Dallas, as promised," Mia assured him.

Ackerman's gaze bounced back and forth between them and though he was clearly not the sharpest knife in the drawer—he'd underestimated *him*, after all—he wasn't as stupid as he looked. There was a wily sort of shrewdness in that pale blue gaze that gave Tanner pause. It wasn't exactly ruthless, but the old reporter clearly had more interest in the exhibit than his story justified.

After a minute, Ackerman nodded to himself and got back into his car, but didn't immediately pull away. A brunette with a bad perm and an overbite sat in the front seat. Tanner made a mental note of the make and model, though, like theirs, it was likely a rental.

Her hand still resting on his arm and fully aware of their continued audience, he turned and made a purely opportunistic but justified decision. He framed her face with his hands and moved in, bellying up to her. "Play along," he whispered, his thumb skimming that insanely sexy bottom lip. Full, lush and rosy, she still had the prettiest mouth he'd ever seen.

Her eyes widened and the hand gripping his arm tightened. "What?"

Tanner tilted her head and brushed his lips over hers, once, twice, slowly savoring the bittersweet feel of her against him once more. He felt her shudder, her breath mingle with his.

The world shifted beneath his feet and he decided that being opportunistic had its advantages.

And if that first taste of her was like a match to kindling, then the second could only be compared to gasoline poured over an open flame—she literally lit him up. The blaze started in the soles of his feet and swept upward, singeing his veins, charring any bit of restraint. One minute, he'd been testing the waters, the next he had her backed up against the hood of the car, his mouth firmly attached to hers.

Mia made a little mewling noise low in her throat, the sound of sweet surrender, and her arms wound around his neck, fitting her petite rounded frame more closely to his. Her hair slithered over the backs of his hands and her tongue tangled around his. In that instant, they could have been twenty again, beneath a library table on campus. She was new and familiar, the same and yet different and, for reasons he couldn't begin to explain, he felt like he'd taken a long and arduous journey only to have finally made it to where he was supposed to be all along. The sensation shook him to the core.

More chick feelings, he thought, shrugging the disconcerting impression away. Dammit, what was wrong with him? And truthfully, he wasn't precisely where he wanted to be. If that were the case, he and Mia would be in a dark room with a big bed and no clock. He would be between her thighs, whispering naughty things in her ear. He dimly noted the sound of Ackerman's car starting and pulling away, and even though the reporter's exit was technically supposed to end their performance, Tanner couldn't find the wherewithal to stop kissing her. She tasted like strawberry jam and minty mouthwash and he wanted to sample the rest of her to test their flavors, as well. He wanted to—

A throat cleared, then, "Mia?"

Mia jolted away from him as though she'd been poked with a cattle prod. Her startled, guilty gaze darted to the left and she rubbed her hand over her mouth, as though she could erase the taste of him. That stung more than it should.

The Boyfriend, Tanner thought, instantly recognizing the guy from the pictures he'd just seen in the apartment.

Shit.

"Harlan," Mia gasped. "I— It's not— This is not what it looks like," she finally managed to say, her voice thin and choppy. She was clearly mortified and it was his fault. *Damn, damn, damn.* They hadn't even made it out of the parking lot yet.

Harlan merely smiled, but his eyes remained cool behind his gold-rimmed glasses. "It's not? Because it looks like you were kissing this guy. Your security agent, I presume?" he asked questioningly. "In the parking lot of my apartment building."

"I was," Mia allowed, dragging the word out as she framed her defense. "But not for the reason you suspect. One of the reporters who's been tailing the exhibit was waiting for me, threatening to follow me to the airport. Tanner played the jealous boyfriend to run him off, but he kept sitting in his car so we…"

"Thought you'd make out?" Harlan suggested helpfully. He crossed his arms over his chest and rocked back on his heels. His gaze slid to Tanner for the first time and a little smirk curled his thin lips. Harlan was a helluva lot quicker than Ackerman, Tanner realized. "No doubt that was your plan."

Mia blinked and her gaze shifted to Tanner. He saw the exact instant when Harlan's implication registered. Her gaze went from melting chocolate—his favorite—to cold brown granite, and her nostrils flared with irritation. She gave a how-could-I-be-so-stupid eye roll and released a tiny sigh.

Tanner heaved a big one.

Admittedly Harlan had a reason to be pissed, but raking Mia over the coals and making her miserable wasn't cool.

Particularly since this was all his fault.

He quirked a brow. "Harlan, is it?"

The guy nodded stiffly.

"Look, Harlan, I made a judgment call and I'm sorry that it's upset you. Yes, I am Mia's security agent, but I can hardly tell anyone that, especially a reporter. I'm sure you understand," he explained, the implication being only a half-wit wouldn't. He shrugged. "Am I sorry for kissing her? No. I'll do whatever I have to do to keep her safe. If that means I stomp on your pride in the process, then so be it. Ultimately, it's not about you."

Harlan paused. "You mean, the statue, don't you?"

"What?"

"You said keep *her* safe. Don't you mean the statue?"

He inwardly swore, belatedly realizing his slip. "They are both under my protection until we reach Dallas." He looked at Mia, who was still quite obviously furious with him. "I'm going to load the car. I'll give you two a minute."

Long enough to say goodbye, but not long enough to resolve anything, Tanner thought.

And the fact that he even cared annoyed the hell out of him.

HARLAN SMILED SADLY. "This isn't working for you, is it?"

"Harlan—"

"Mia, you don't have to deny it. You're six shades of red and only three of them account for the shamefaced blush. You've had one foot out the door for months now. Don't insult my intelligence by pretending otherwise."

Impossibly, she felt her face flame even hotter. She looked away, watching a little house sparrow scamper around and peck a crack in the sidewalk. "I, uh…"

What could she say? He was right. If he hadn't walked up and interrupted them, who knew what would have happened? She doubted they'd have dropped onto the pavement and gone at it right there, but moving things into the car had certainly been a possibility.

To her absolute chagrin, she'd had no thought of stopping.

In fact, she'd been too busy *feeling* to do anything else.

The thick, hot rush of desire. The warm muddled sensation in her belly. The tingly heat pulsing in her nipples. The deep, rhythmic throbbing in her weeping sex. All of it combined with the exquisite sensation of his mouth feeding at hers, those big, strong hands sliding over her body, framing her face. She shivered anew, remembering, and let out a shallow breath. It had been *so* long...

When she looked up, Harlan was smiling at her, confirmation of his suspicions in his eyes. "I'm sorry, Harlan," she said, wincing with regret.

He slid a finger down her cheek. "I am, too, but that doesn't change the outcome, does it? I know how to recognize an exit scene and this is mine."

He jerked his head toward the car, where Tanner waited. Impatiently, by the look of it, which served him right. Self-serving bastard. Sneaky sonofabitch. She couldn't believe he'd taken advantage of her like that.

"I can't compete with that," Harlan finished.

Mia swallowed, uncomfortably aware of how much she was botching this. Harlan was a good man—not the right one for her, sadly—but good all the same and she didn't like making him feel small. "It isn't a competition."

He looked away, seeming to choose his words carefully. "It can't be if I take myself out of it." He stepped back and sent Tanner a speculative glance. "Be careful with this guy, Mia. That's the trouble with fire. It burns."

And with that parting advice, he brushed a kiss against her cheek, then turned and walked away.

Though she'd known this was the only possibly outcome, that the relationship was never going to be anything more than lukewarm and comfortable, she nevertheless wouldn't have chosen to end things this way. She could have let Harlan down gently, left him with a little bit of dignity. They would have discussed it like rational, mature adults, come to the mutual agreement that things weren't working and parted ways. He wouldn't have had to witness her practically velcroed to Tanner, making out like a couple of hormone-happy teenagers with no curfew and a hot condom at the ready.

She turned and glared daggers at Tanner through the windshield of the car.

Follow my lead.

She could cheerfully throttle him.

Mia pushed her hair away from her still-burning face, turned on her heel and made her way to the car. She pulled the handle up, but the latch held. Her nail didn't. She inhaled sharply at the pain, then looked at her wrecked manicure and felt the childish urge to stamp her foot like a thwarted toddler. A frustrated scream built in the back of her throat and it took every ounce of control she possessed to keep it down to a mere growl.

This was his fault, too, she thought furiously, pulling the rest of the ruined nail from her finger. Idiot man. What kind of security specialist locked the person he was supposed to be protecting *out* of the car? Brilliant, right? She heard the telltale click of the lock tumble back, then jerked the door open and flung herself into the passenger seat. "Way to protect me, genius," she said, her voice tight. "I can't say that I'm familiar with the old locking-your-target-out-of-the-car procedure."

She had the pleasure of watching his cheeks flush. Irritatingly, it only made him more handsome. "Sorry," he muttered. "I'm not used to this car."

Without bothering to look at him, she dug a nail file from her purse and tried to smooth the rough edges from her index finger. "And yet that doesn't inspire confidence."

He slipped the gearshift into Reverse and smoothly backed out of the space, before dropping it into Drive and hitting the accelerator. Tires squealed as they darted off and she felt the small of her back land firmly against the seat. Show off, she thought, hating the fact that her pulse kicked up. A competent driver had always turned her on.

"Furthermore," he said, his voice tight. "My primary concern is Dick, not you, and he was never in any danger." He grimaced at her hand and swallowed. "I'm sorry about your nail."

She whirled on him, her mouth dropping open in

outraged shock. "You're sorry about my nail? *My nail?* You tricked me into kissing you, my boyfriend saw and now we've broken up. And you're *sorry about my nail?*" She rested against the seat once more and shook her head at his gall. "That's rich, Tanner."

Tanner shot her a look. "He broke up with you? Over that? Seriously?"

She snorted under her breath. "Follow my lead, my ass," she muttered, still in a state of shock. "And I did, fool that I am." She gave her head a disbelieving shake, still stunned at her own stupidity. "I am a complete and utter moron."

"Don't be so hard on yourself," he advised, to her astonishment, quite seriously. "I might have played you a little bit, but I had no idea that your boyfriend would catch us." He negotiated a turn, one that would put them on the interstate soon. "And since it didn't occur to you, either, I don't see how you can hold me accountable for that."

It was hard to argue with that kind of logic, though she desperately wished she could. Damn him for being right. She hadn't thought once of Harlan when Tanner had kissed her. Hadn't spared her boyfriend a thought, formed even a token protest. There was something quite telling in that, but she was too busy being irritated at Tanner to think it through properly.

Her brooding gaze slid to his profile, taking in the lean lines of his face, the easy competent grace in his hands as he handled the car. Hands that had just as competently handled her just a few minutes ago. A rush of warmth pooled in her middle and her palms literally itched to touch him again, to feel every perfectly proportioned inch of him beneath her fingers. She massaged the bridge of her nose and released another tiny sigh.

"You okay?" He slid her a nervous look. "You aren't going to cry, are you?"

Because he looked so comically worried, Mia toyed with the idea of producing a few tears, but ultimately dismissed it. "No," she said, heaving a sigh. She dropped her head back against the seat and relaxed more fully. "I'm not going to cry."

"Girls usually cry when they break up with their boyfriends."

Her lips twitched in a sad effort at a smile. "This girl knew it was coming."

A beat slid to three as he seemed to wrestle with asking her what she meant. It was a personal question and, though she knew he wasn't averse to getting personal with her on a physical level, getting into the sticky details of her love life was something else altogether. Just when she was convinced that he wasn't going to ask, he did. In a voice that was just as grudging as it was reluctant. He didn't *like* wanting to know and, for whatever reason, that burst a little bubble of happiness inside her.

He drummed his fingers impatiently against the steering wheel. "Why did you know it was coming?"

She shrugged. "Things have felt a bit off for a while."

Okay, so that was sort of truthful. She didn't have

to tell him that they'd never felt particularly on. That something—a key component—had always been missing. Mia had thought that being friends would be enough, that being with a like-minded person with the same interests and values would suffice. It had come as quite a shock to her when she realized it wouldn't. When the lack of physical compatibility had become a real issue.

He inclined his head knowingly. "Ah. In the bedroom?"

She turned to glare at him, irritated at his presumptive but annoyingly correct assumption. As though all she needed from a man was a good roll in the sack.

"No," she denied, exasperated. "Harlan is a spectacular lover," she lied baldly, suddenly hit with the uncontrollable urge to needle him, to make him pay for the scene outside the apartment building. She smiled and twisted a lock of hair around her finger, pretending to recall a certain magical memory. She chuckled low and gave her head a small shake. "No, the bedroom was where we went when everything else was going wrong. That sure as hell wasn't the problem."

Clearly that was not the answer Tanner had been expecting to hear. His facial expression had blanked and his lips had turned down at the corners, as though he'd smelled something bad. She gave a little inward cheer.

"So what then?" he asked, his voice curiously flat. "You belong to different political parties? He liked forking better than spooning? He wasn't intellectually stimulating enough?"

"F-forking better t-than spooning?" she repeated, snickering under her breath. "That's a new one."

"You didn't answer me," he told her.

He took the exit for sixty-six west, merging seamlessly into the heavy flow of traffic. He kept a careful watch in the rearview mirror, constantly taking stock of their surroundings. She got the feeling that if she asked him about the make and model of the car five lengths behind them, he'd be able to tell her without hesitating. Though he gave the impression of effortless unconcern, she knew beyond a shadow of a doubt that those keen eyes weren't missing a thing.

"That's because I don't know exactly," she finally answered. She picked at a lose thread on the hem of her shirt. "On the surface, he was perfect. Steady, stable, loyal."

A sardonic grin curled his lips. "Like a golden retriever."

"No, like a good man is supposed to be," she said simply. "There's a lot to be said for a guy who doesn't bolt, who wants a home and family. He's smart and funny and like I said, the sex was *phenomenal.*"

"So you've said," he muttered tightly. A muscle jumped in his tense jaw. "But?"

But he couldn't light me up, Mia thought. He didn't make her feel like she was plugged into an electrical outlet. He didn't make her long for lazy Sundays in bed, for impulsive sex in inconvenient moments. She'd never looked across the table at him and thought "Damn it all, I've got to have you right friggin' *now*." There was no urgency, no ultimate immediacy, no flare.

In short, sadly, he didn't make her glow.

Unfortunately the only guy who'd ever done that was the one sitting next to her. And he had "temporary" stamped in invisible ink all over him. Holding on to Tanner would be like trying to hold on to air—impossible.

She sighed heavily, but not for the reason he would think. "But...we didn't have that special spark," she finally said. "We clicked, but could never quite fit the pieces together the way they were supposed to go."

He inclined his head, but didn't offer comment. His gaze shifted to the rearview mirror and he swore.

"What?" Mia asked, instantly on alert.

"I know that I am poor substitute for Harlan," he said, his lips twisting with bitter humor. "But you didn't mind kissing me too much, did you?"

"No," she admitted suspiciously. "Why?"

"Because Ackerman is following us. If I can't shake him, we're probably going to have to give him an encore performance."

She gulped and the tops of her thighs burned. "All the way to Dallas?"

"Quite possibly." He didn't look broken up about it at all. In fact, gratifyingly, he looked quite keen on the idea.

She heaved a put-upon sigh, even while that damned wicked thrill whipped her insides into a froth of sexual delight. "Well, I suppose I have to go along with it now," she told him grudgingly. "We've already set the stage, so to speak."

And her libido, dammit, was fully on cue.

5

THIS WAS THE PART HE loved the most, he thought. The thrill of a new mystery, a potentially worthy adversary. After all, anything worth having was worth fighting for. Who was the man Mia had left with? he wondered. What was his part in all of this? Was he the boyfriend? No, definitely not. The man his source had described didn't remotely resemble Professor Harlan Carmichael. His source had yet to uncover the name for the new man, but when he got it, he would have his answers. It was amazing what one could find on the Internet these days.

Furthermore, the presence of a backpack, one the man seemed quite protective of, offered a myriad of new possibilities.

Best not to get too far ahead of himself, he thought. He would be patient and await further information. Acting rashly, no matter how tempting it might be, could end in disaster.

But he was watching....

"Is this really necessary?" Mia hissed later that evening as Tanner handed his company credit card over to the hotel clerk. "We have to stay in the same room?"

Tanner had anticipated the shared accommodation to be an issue, but he wasn't willing to compromise the job because of her need for privacy. She was going to simply think he was opportunistic and, though he was willing to admit keeping her close was a certain perk, ultimately it wouldn't have mattered if she'd been the denture clicker he'd originally envisioned. This was how it had to be.

The end.

"I got a double. You'll have your own bed."

"But—"

Tanner straightened and turned to face her, casually assessing the room around them. He'd chosen this particular brand of hotel because it was the easiest to monitor and offered the most expedient escape route should they need it. It was one time when cookie-cutter architecture was actually good. Their subsequent rooms were prebooked, as well. "Here's the deal, Mia," he said. "I'm not letting Moe Dick leave my sight and you aren't willing to let him leave yours, are you?"

She shook her head, obviously realizing that whatever argument she was about to launch was useless. "No, of course not."

"Then this is the only way we're both going to be satisfied."

Satisfied? Poor choice of words, he thought, his lips twisting with weary humor. He wouldn't be satisfied until he was deep in the sweet hot channel between her sweet thighs, eradicating Harlan's *Super Lover* status from her stubborn, clearly misinformed little brain. Either she'd forgotten how competitive he was or she hadn't, and was purposely torturing him.

Either way, he still wanted her.

And to think, just yesterday morning he'd told his new employers that there wouldn't be any possibility that he could impregnate Mia. The backpack suddenly felt heavier on his shoulders at the thought. But even with the best intentions, he should have known better.

She'd always lit him up.

That had been part of the problem and no small part of the reason he'd broken up with her. In addition to those softer, weaker emotions he'd never liked feeling when he was around her—or hell, away from her for that matter—there'd always been a humming, undercurrent of almost-irresistible need between them, one that no amount of discipline could smother. He hadn't just wanted her—he'd had to have her. As though being joined with her was the only place in the world he needed to be, the only place on the planet he could ever feel truly at peace. At rest. And considering the state of him right now, when he was getting precious little sleep and rest was a rare commodity…

Damn.

That's why he'd ultimately broken things off between them. He'd needed her too much, had wanted her too much, depended on her too much for his own happiness. He'd craved her company beyond anything and it had absolutely terrified him. He'd had a reputation for being fearless even then, but the feelings she'd unwittingly engendered in him had put the fear of God into him, that was for sure. His gaze slid over the smooth slope of her cheek, the adorable upturned nose.

Truth be told, he was rattled to the core even now and he would have thought—especially after what he'd seen outside Mosul—he was well past the point of having his cage shaken.

"You're right," she said suddenly, surprising him. She shook her head and shot him a wan smile. "I'm being ridiculous. It's late, we're tired. I don't know about you, but I just want to eat, shower and go to bed."

Tanner merely grunted. It sounded like an excellent plan to him. Shaking Ackerman hadn't been too much of a challenge—he'd been Ranger, for God's sake, one of the best trained soldiers in the world. The day he couldn't evade a middle-aged reporter in a beat-up sedan was the day he ate his beret.

Nevertheless, between constantly scoping out the rearview mirror and the ceaseless current of sexual awareness—one that seemed impossibly more potent than he remembered—he was pretty damned exhausted himself. Dinner, a hot shower—or more likely a cold one, he amended, taking a glance at Mia's especially carnal mouth—and hitting a soft mattress sounded damned good indeed. Maybe he'd get a few solid hours of sleep before the inevitable nightmares started. His gaze slid to Mia.

And that presented another problem. He'd have to tell

her about them. As vaguely as possible, of course, but he couldn't very well just forget to mention that at some point during the night, he'd sit bolt upright, screaming. He'd scare her to death.

"Here's your key," the clerk said, handing him the small envelope, making a point to touch him in the process. Her voice was slightly breathless and the flirtatious look she was giving him was bad form considering he was checking in with another woman. He was flattered, of course, but come on. She was practically hitting on him right in front of Mia.

From the corner of his eye, he saw Mia expel an annoyed breath.

For whatever reason, that telling little gesture made something in his chest expand with masculine pleasure.

Continuing to act as though Mia didn't exist, the clerk gave him brief instructions on how to find their room. She needn't have bothered—he knew exactly where it was. He'd requested it, after all, when he'd made the reservation. Fidgeting, the clerk bit her lip and looked at him from beneath lowered lashes. "We don't offer room service, but The Pancake Barn next door has a decent menu and will deliver for a small fee. Let me know if I can get anything for you." She leaned forward, purposely accentuating her cleavage. "Anything at all."

"I'm good, thanks," Tanner said, bemused at her behavior. "That was weird."

Mia shrugged, fatalistically. "That's Moe."

He blinked, startled. Moe? "What?"

She rolled her eyes. "Oh, come on, Tanner. I know you're a good-looking guy and you're used to making minimal effort to attract a woman, but do you honestly think that woman would have been so blatant about wanting to hook up with you, especially with me standing there, if it wasn't for Moe?"

Moe? *Moe?* What did he have to do with this? Surely she didn't mean— He felt his jaw drop. "You have *got* to be kidding me. You mean, you actually believe all that crap? All the hype surrounding that little statue?" He snugged his fingers into the small of her back and guided her through the lobby, past the potted palms and hospitality area, then down the hall, where their room would be the last on the right, nearest the exit.

"Doesn't matter what he's made of," she said matter-of-factly. "He works."

He couldn't believe it. Couldn't believe she, of all people, *Ms. Logic,* genuinely bought into this load of sh—

She waited for him to fish the key out of the envelope and open the door. "You're telling me you didn't notice that guy coming on to me at the restaurant we stopped at in Harrisonburg? What? You think I always get that kind of attention?"

As a matter of fact, he did. She was gorgeous. Why wouldn't any guy trip over himself to get to her? And he *had* noticed the pimply-faced teen practically drooling all over her at Cracker Barrel. He'd just chalked it up to the fact that her mouth looked like it belonged under a street lamp and the clingy knit top she was wearing showcased a world-class pair of breasts. She was uncommonly hot, unassumingly beautiful and refreshingly ignorant of her own appeal.

But Moe? Nah… He just didn't buy it.

Stale air and the scent of bathroom cleaner greeted them as he pushed open the door. Two double beds as promised, mounded with pillows and good linens, a nice desk with a good lamp and a decent flat-panel television. Generic floral paintings in bold colors hung behind the beds, the only nod to décor. The bathroom was nice, with granite countertops. A small coffeepot with all the proper accoutrements sat next to the usual array of hotel toiletries. It wasn't the Ritz, but it would do.

"And all those couples who were sitting around us?" she continued. "Didn't you notice how they scooted their chairs closer together? How the conversation got more intimate and low? At a Cracker Barrel," she emphasized with a significant widening of her eyes. And he had to admit, she had a good point.

The country restaurant and store wasn't exactly known for its romantic atmosphere. It offered good food at reasonable prices with an added perk of having a store attached. It was not the sort of place that offered cozy, quiet dining. Still, he just couldn't make himself believe it, couldn't bring himself to even imagine a world where a fertility statue would actually work. It was too far-fetched. Too far out of the realm of possibility.

"Then there's the kiss we had this afternoon," she continued, plopping herself down on the end of the bed.

"Do you really think either one of us would have gotten so carried away if it hadn't been for Moe?"

Okay, dammit. He was drawing the line right there. He set their luggage aside and shrugged out of the backpack, then chuckled darkly. "Oh, I don't know. I seem to recall that we used to enjoy kissing each other a lot."

She flushed, but her gaze stayed steady. "True," she conceded levelly. "But that was before you dumped me like yesterday's garbage and avoided eye contact right up until the day we graduated. Then, of course, you went off to parts unknown." She lay back and stretched her toes. "Believe me, Tanner, if it wasn't for Moe, you wouldn't have had such a welcome reception this morning, Ackerman or no Ackerman."

Great. So not only was Harlan the best lover she'd ever had, he had Moe to thank for her enthusiastic response to his kiss this morning.

In other words, she was attracted to him because of Moe.

How galling.

Seemingly unaware of the blow she'd just delivered to his ego, she turned to him with a plaintive expression. "Do you mind if I use the shower first? I feel icky."

He shook his head and his gaze slid to the backpack. He began to genuinely dislike the little statue. "No, not at all. I need to boot up my laptop and check a few things." All true, but he also needed to cool down. Anymore of this conversation and he might just decide to rectify some of her false assumptions, beginning with a quick tumble onto the bed.

With a grateful sigh, she gathered her toiletry bag, a gown and robe and disappeared into the bathroom. In an effort to focus on anything but thoughts of her naked body, Tanner withdrew his computer from its case and set to work, which was supposed to be his primary focus anyway.

He had a job to do, dammit, and whether or not Mia's interest in him stemmed from Moe or from true chemistry, that didn't change. He needed to remember that.

Thanks to the resources made available to him through Ranger Security, he knew that Ackerman had been booked onto the same flight as Mia. What had prompted the reporter to want to "follow" her to the airport? Tanner wondered. What had tipped him off to the fact that she wasn't going to be on that plane? Or had he just been following a hunch? Somehow Tanner didn't think so.

Furthermore, though he'd noticed him at the museum, Ramirez had faded to black, as it were. Because he was wealthy enough to avoid commercial travel, Ramirez had his own private plane. It had been scheduled for departure from Reagan International this afternoon and a quick check confirmed that it had left on schedule. But was Ramirez aboard? Or had he found an alternate means of transportation, as well? One that would make him more of a threat than he already was.

On the surface, this seemed like a fairly simple mission. Safely move Moe Dick and the museum liaison from Point A to Point B. But when one considered that Moe Dick had a wily reporter following his every move, a ruthless, wealthy treasure hunter who was determined to add the little statue to his collection and an old girlfriend who still had the ability to set his loins on fire and kindle a more terrifying reaction in his heart, this became a quagmire of the first order.

The box of condoms Jamie had tossed him peeked out from the corner of his laptop case, mocking him in the process.

He suddenly realized why the former Rangers had been so concerned.

He was screwed.

CONFIDENT THAT TANNER HAD everything under control, Mia escaped to the bathroom to try and regain her composure a little. She carefully set her things on the vanity, taking care to leave some room for Tanner for his toiletries and stowed her too-short robe on a hook on the back of the door. The ritual didn't completely calm her nerves, but it kept her hands busy and, at the moment, she needed to do something to keep them off the man on the other side of the door.

Honestly, though she knew it could just be her imagination—and it probably was—she could have sworn she felt some sort of heat rising from the backpack. She'd been more aware of Moe and his enormous genitalia than she ever had been before and was convinced, more now than ever about his power. Every particle of her body had been hammeringly aware of Tanner today and, while she'd admit that her reaction wasn't surprising, she'd never imagined that her awareness of him would be so strong, almost irresistible.

She'd only been one pothole or speed bump away from an immaculate orgasm for most of the their journey, and they were only in Roanoke. They had many miles and many hours to go. There was no way in hell she was going to survive this without coming unglued.

Or mentally unhinged.

In light of that, Mia carefully disrobed, turned on the tap and adjusted the temperature to suit her purposes. The bathroom had a detachable massaging showerhead and Mia had never been more thankful for a modern convenience. She braced one foot against the side of the tub, hiking her leg, and aimed the hot pulsing spray at the area that needed the most attention.

In mere seconds, the pressurized water had done the trick and she could feel a portion of the tension leaking out of her body. Not enough, of course—she needed some real, back-clawing, belly-shivering, toe-curling, mind-numbing sex for that—but, despite what her body wanted, it would have to do.

In all fairness, she had a perfect excuse in Moe to take Tanner back into her bed. She could quite easily blame every bit of this miserable attraction on him. Tanner, though annoyed, would never be any the wiser. After all, she'd just set the stage for that, and she had to admit, seeing his slightly stricken expression had been quite gratifying. Mia had too much pride to tell him the truth—that, sexually, he'd always set the standard—and too much self-respect and self-preservation to simply let him waltz back into her life, or more accurately, into her body.

He'd dumped her, she reminded herself. He'd broken her heart. She shouldn't want him. She shouldn't ache to ask him a million questions about his life. Had he ever married? Did he have children? Had the military been all he'd imagined? Was his father proud of him?

That had been another goal, one that she knew Tanner had held just as dear as the others. He'd constantly cited his father's military career with a sense of pride and longing in his voice. He'd desperately wanted to live up to the elder Crawford's expectations. Even then, Mia had wondered if that had been an attainable goal. Though she'd only met the retired major once, it had been enough to see the strain on the relationship between the two men.

She also wondered if Tanner still read Shakespeare? Or had he ever been to Baltimore to see the Poe Toaster?

He'd mentioned doing that several times when they'd been together, she recalled now. Given that the Poe Toaster hadn't made an appearance this year—the first time since nineteen-forty-nine that the bottle of cognac and three roses weren't left on Edgar Allen Poe's original grave on his birthday—she wondered if that would be something Tanner would ever get to see, if he hadn't already. She had dozens of questions, but pride kept her from asking. It was better for Tanner to think she didn't care, that she had truly been ready to call it quits between them when he did.

The most pressing question, of course, was why had he left the military? Though she'd originally noted that his eyes were the same, upon closer inspection, she'd had to amend her opinion. True, they were the same color, but there was a strain around them now, a world-weary knowledge of things she'd never seen, etched into the fine lines around those unusual orbs. He looked... haunted, for a lack of better description, Mia noted, and that undue weariness tugged at her heart.

The only thing that hadn't changed was his ability to absolutely turn her inside out. Just looking at him made her heart ache in her chest, made her stomach bob around like a worm wriggling on a hook. The combination of affection and attraction simply slayed her, even now. She'd never felt anything like it, anything even remotely close since they'd been together. Even with all the water under the bridge. Frankly, she would have thought their years apart would have washed away whatever feelings she had for him. But one look was all it had taken to resurrect every single tender feeling she'd ever had for him, make her remember his every touch against her skin. The want, the need, the breathless anticipation of his kiss, of that perfect moment when their two bodies became one.

It was grossly unfair, Mia thought, the supreme height of injustice. Clearly he'd moved on. And for all intents and purposes, she had, too. She had her career, one that she loved. And she loved her little craftsman-style home in Savannah, another sign of progression. She'd painstakingly restored the bulk of it herself, stripping floors, sanding windowsills and cleaning the fireplaces. Her cheeks puffed as she exhaled mightily.

And until today she'd had a boyfriend. Admittedly, Harlan had been on his way out, but still, he'd been there. He hadn't necessarily been a placeholder for someone better, but…what exactly had been their relationship? In all honesty, she didn't know. She just knew that the only man she'd ever truly cared for and truly, desperately wanted was on the other side of the wall.

And that, unfortunately for her heart, was too damned close for comfort.

In order to save him a bit of hot water, Mia hurried through the rest of her shower and quickly ran through her nightly routine. Her hands shook as she belted the sash to her robe and she expelled a shaky breath before finally opening the door.

Tanner had ordered food from next door and a carry-out tray was sitting on her bed.

He looked up when she came out and she felt the slide of his gaze traipse slowly over her frame. "I hope you don't mind, but I went ahead and ordered us a couple of sandwiches and fries."

She nodded and picked up the container, surprised at how hungry she actually was. Of course, she'd used up a lot of energy lusting after him today, so… "That's fine, thanks."

He popped a fry into his mouth. "No mustard, no pickle on your hamburger, right?"

He remembered that? "Er…right. Thanks."

"How's the shower?" he asked.

Her head jerked up and she felt a guilty flush slide over her cheeks. Did he know? How could he know? She hadn't even moaned. "Hot," she said cautiously, sliding him a look.

"A good, strong spray?" he asked.

Strong enough, she thought, deliberately opening a packet of ketchup. She cleared her throat, felt her lips twitch. "Yeah, I think so. It felt good to me, anyway."

"Excellent," he told her, popping another French fry into his mouth. "I hate those weak jobs."

Belatedly she realized he was nervous, that he seemed to be trying to fill the air with words. Either the silence offended him, or he was trying to work up the nerve to tell her something else. Knowing Tanner as she did, her money was on the latter.

He rubbed his hand over the back of his neck. "Listen, Mia..."

So she was right, Mia thought, bracing herself. She turned to look at him and quirked a brow. He looked adorably unsure, an odd expression on a face that was usually so confident. "Yes?"

He hesitated. "I wouldn't tell you this unless I had to, but since we're sleeping in the same room and I don't want you to be afraid—" he winced regrettably "—I don't really see any other way around it."

Curiosity spiked to fever pitch. "Tell me what?"

"If I yell or thrash around in my sleep, just give me a sharp jab, okay? Just a quick poke to wake me up."

She felt a frown furrow her brow. Yell or thrash around? "You mean, like a nightmare?"

The shame on his face was utterly unmistakable and equally heart-wrenching. "Something like that, yes."

Nightmares of what? Of war? she wondered, figuring that was the most likely answer. Her own heart gave a little squeeze and, though her first instinct was to lay a hand on his and comfort him, she knew that wasn't what he needed. And he damned sure didn't need her asking a lot of questions.

She merely nodded, purposely keeping it light. "Sure."

Seemingly relieved that the subject was closed, he polished off the last bite of his burger. He picked up Moe and slung him over his shoulder. "I'm going to jump in the shower."

Her lips twitched. "You're taking Moe?"

"I'm not supposed to let him out of my sight." His gaze grew speculative. "Or you, either, technically. Come on," he said. "Bring a book and you can sit on the commode."

Mia smiled. "You're joking, right?"

"No," he said, though she caught a telltale twinkle in his eye. "It's standard procedure."

"I'll take my chances," Mia told him.

"Fine," he said. "Stubborn, disagreeable woman," he muttered.

"I imagine any woman who doesn't do exactly what you want is labeled 'stubborn' and 'disagreeable.'"

A slow smile shaped his lips. "To tell you the truth, I don't run into many of those."

She felt the tops of her ears burn. Of course, he

wouldn't. He would "run into" the kinds of women who threw themselves at him, who didn't have any expectations, who didn't want anything more from him than a couple of drinks and a quick roll in the hay.

She *hated* those women, each and every slutty one of them.

"Then this is going to be a novel experience for you then," she said, lifting her chin.

To her surprise, Tanner guffawed. "On my first assignment for Ranger Security I'm traveling with a former girlfriend and a fertility statue with purported magical powers, which is under threat from a variety of difference sources. That's *novel*," he said. "You being stubborn and disagreeable is the only thing about this trip that's *not* unique."

Mia grinned, despite herself. "Smart-ass."

"See what I mean," he said, gesturing as if she herself were evidence. "This is what I mean about you. I knew you were going to offer some sort of comment like that."

"Clearly, I am going to have to work at being less predictable then."

He passed a hand over his face and shook his head. "I'd rather you didn't."

"Because you like that I'm predictable?"

"Because I like you," he said simply, and the unexpected compliment reverberated pleasantly through her. "I'm getting in the shower. Don't open the door for anyone." He paused as though a thought had struck. "Have you ever fired a gun?"

"No."

If she'd said "I like to kill puppies for fun" he couldn't have looked any more shocked. "You don't even have one for protection?"

She shook her head. "I've got a baseball bat at home and a can of Mace in my purse."

He grimaced and she watched him retrieve the handgun from its holster. "Keep the Mace handy," he instructed. He bent down and carefully put the gun in her hand, closing his fingers around hers. "This is the safety," he explained.

"Yep. I've heard of those." The weapon felt cool and heavy against her palm. Solid.

"You're going to take it off, like this," he said, demonstrating for her benefit. "Then you're ready to fire."

She gulped and her hand began to shake. "You mean, it's loaded."

He smiled, his eyes crinkling around the corners. That smile tugged at something in her belly. He was so close she could smell his cologne again. Yum. "It's not much use otherwise, is it?"

"Well, no, but…" She bit her lip. "Do I really need to know this?"

"You should have already known this," he told her, censure leaking into his tone. "You need to know how to protect yourself."

His advice was definitely ironic, coming from the only man who'd ever truly hurt her, Mia thought. Her heart had felt like it had been put through a wood chipper after he'd gotten through with it. It had taken years to put it back together. But, ultimately, she knew that wasn't what he was talking about. Point of fact, she'd had friends tell her as much and knew that he was right.

Better safe than sorry.

And that was a sentiment she desperately needed to keep in mind over the next few days.

6

THOUGH HE'D TAKEN EVERY precaution he could think of, and had scanned the immediate area of the hotel many times, Tanner couldn't shake the uncomfortable sensation that they were being watched. Call it gut instinct, a premonition or the onset of sudden psychic ability, the end result was always the same.

Someone was watching them. He could feel it.

Initially, he had to admit that he'd sort of thought this mission was a joke—certainly there was lots of potential for humor when one was guarding a large, stone penis—but the actual seriousness of the situation suddenly hit him like a ton of bricks.

Ackerman's showing up at Mia's apartment should have been enough of a clue, yet it hadn't set off the warning bells it had truly warranted. How had Ackerman known where Mia was staying? The address wouldn't have been in any research the man could have come across. It was Harlan's apartment, after all. Obviously the reporter had either followed her there or had gotten information from an inside source. The former was more likely, he thought, and the idea of the sneaky little man scuttling furtively behind Mia made his blood boil.

Yet Mia seemed to regard the older reporter with a strange sort of tolerant fondness, one he admittedly didn't understand. When he'd asked her about it, she'd insisted that Freddie was enthusiastic, but harmless, that he was more of a nuisance than anything else. But Tanner wasn't so sure.

His gaze slid to Mia, who was calmly reading the paper while she sipped her coffee. There was a swan-like grace about her, Tanner noted, in the way she tilted her head, in the smooth economy of movement in her slim hands. A sleepy flush still clung to her cheeks, like rosy porcelain, and contrasted beautifully with her dark, shiny hair. Occasionally she'd read something that made her frown or provoked a slight upturn of her mouth and he found himself suddenly desperate to know what was going on in that head of hers, what had prompted those intriguing expressions. He'd stopped himself twice from asking her what she was thinking—the single most invasive question there ever was, one he'd never felt compelled to ask before—and berated himself for wanting to know. He shouldn't care, dammit. Ultimately what she thought or didn't think, didn't matter. He had a job to do, a life to put back together.

This morning she'd laced her hair into a single thick braid that hung over her right shoulder and she'd dressed in a clingy bright green shirt that showcased the most beautiful breasts he'd ever seen. Just looking at them made his mouth water, made him want to nose the fabric aside and nuzzle the valley in between.

She made his blood run hot for another reason altogether, he thought broodingly, and that was no doubt why he'd failed to see the obvious yesterday. How humiliating. He'd had years of training, hours and hours of elite military conditioning and he'd missed something so glaringly obvious because seeing her again had turned him inside out.

Intellect told him he should call Payne and tell him he needed to get another agent on this case ASAP, that he should excuse himself from the mission at once based on his personal history with Mia. Hell, he should have done it the minute he'd seen her picture. Or better still, when Jamie had tossed him the box of condoms.

Unfortunately, intellect was no match for his pride and that substantial ego combined with the genuine fear that they'd fire him, leaving him nowhere to go, kept him from making that call.

He absolutely could not fail here. Landing this job had been the one thing that had made him feel like he wasn't the washed-up disgrace his father had accused him of being.

You're weak. You disgust me. Your grandfather and I handed you a heritage and you've dishonored it.

Tanner had known when he made the agonizing decision to leave the military that he'd incur his father's derision, but he hadn't worried about losing the old man's good opinion. His lips twisted bitterly. How could you lose what you'd never had in the first place?

No success—be it in the classroom, on the football field or in the military—had ever been met with a single "atta-boy." Criticism on the other hand? There'd always been plenty of that to go around.

In light of his father's habitual fault-finding, Tanner had always discounted his commentary. But because there was a nugget of truth in this instance, the ridicule had struck a nerve. He'd even avoided contacting his grandfather, afraid that the old man would share his father's opinion.

And, ultimately John Crawford's was the only one that had ever truly mattered.

Seeing disappointment in his father's face was nothing new, familiar even. But seeing it in his grandfather's was another matter altogether and Tanner wasn't certain he could handle it. He would at some point, of course. He couldn't forsake his family forever—at least the ones who wanted to see him, like his mother and sister. His grandfather, too, he knew. But Tanner had to admit, he was worried about looking the old man in the eye, was afraid of what he'd see there.

The same could be said when he looked in the mirror, for that matter.

Between the shame, the guilt and the nightmares, finding his way back to his former self—if that was even possible—was proving to be damned arduous, much more so than he'd imagined. He'd caught a glimmer of that guy when Colonel Garrett had told him about Ranger Security and knew that this job was an integral part of redefining his purpose.

That Mia was along for the ride, quite honestly, was a bad piece of luck he could have done without. A reunion in any other circumstances would have been welcome, but now? *Troublesome, distracting* and *potentially disastrous* came immediately to mind.

As did *hot, frantic* and *cataclysmic*.

Sheesh.

"What?" Mia asked, in the process of slathering cream cheese onto a toasted bagel.

Confused, Tanner looked at her. "What do you mean what?"

"You grunted," she said.

So he had, but he hadn't spoken. He arched a baffled brow.

"What did it mean?"

Mean? He still wasn't following. "The grunt?"

"Yes," she said, slightly exasperated. She opened a small tub of strawberry jam and smeared it on top of the cream cheese. "It sounded fatalistic, a little disgusted."

Tanner chuckled. "You got all of that from a grunt?"

"Men articulate more through grunts, groans and growls than through actual language. Much like apes," she added, hiding her smile behind her coffee cup. "That grunt could have meant anything from 'Damn, I missed *Baywatch* last night' to 'Pity no one has discovered a cure for cancer.'"

Tanner smothered a grin. "I'll put your mind at ease then. I wasn't thinking either one of those thoughts.

Like apes," he muttered with an eye roll, once again struck by her bizarre sense of humor. "Tell me something," he said. "Have you ever noticed Ackerman following you before? Seen him hanging around Harlan's apartment?"

She mulled it over. "No, not that I've noticed."

"Had you ever told him where you were staying?"

Her gaze sharpened. "No, definitely not."

"Could he have found out through anyone close to you? Your assistant, perhaps? Other employees working the exhibit?"

A frown knitted her brow. "I can't imagine that anyone working the exhibit, my personal assistant included, would give out that kind of information about me. Sophie and the others were staying at a hotel near the museum and it was common knowledge among staff that I was staying at Harlan's. But none of them would have any reason to divulge that information." Her keen gaze searched his. "Why do you ask?"

"Because Ackerman found you there yesterday," Tanner told her. "How did he know you were there? Did someone tip him off or did he follow you?"

From the look on her face, neither scenario was pleasing. "If I had to guess, I'd say he followed me," Mia finally said. She glanced out the window and froze, a strange look capturing her face.

"Something wrong?" Tanner asked, going on instant alert.

She continued to peer out the window, then turned to look at him, her expression not readily readable. "No," she said, still frowning. "I thought I saw my fath—" She shook her head, dismissing whatever idea had taken root there. "I'm being ridiculous. Never mind," she told him. "Back to Ackerman. It's possible that he went to the hotel where the rest of the staff were booked and watched enough to know that I wasn't with them, but…"

Tanner scanned the parking lot, looking for whatever Mia had thought she'd seen. The lot was empty, the cars unattended. Mildly satisfied, he found her gaze once more. "If he'd gotten Harlan's name, he could have easily pulled the address. Who on site knows of Ranger Security's involvement?"

"Just Ed Thompson, of course, and Sophie." Her steady gaze found his. "And before you even suggest it, I trust both of them implicitly."

The museum had run their own extensive background checks and had cleared each worker. Then Ranger Security had performed an even deeper search. But there was only so much information that could be found through the usual channels. While a good check could paint a picture of a person's life, character and immediate circumstances, motivation could be sadly lacking and unfortunately, that's the sort of information they needed. Ramirez was a collector who thought the statue should be rightfully his—his interest was explainable. But Ackerman?

Furthermore, Ramirez was too smart to act himself. His M.O. was to have dispensable henchmen in place who, for a price, would be willing to risk imprisonment.

Those shadowy figures were the ones Tanner needed to identify, to run background checks on because ultimately, *they* were the direct threat.

The Head of Security seemed solid enough, but Sophie hadn't come across as reliable, in his opinion. Eager? Yes. Even competent. But she had an unmistakable lack of maturity that he found a bit worrisome. It was entirely possible that she'd unintentionally let something slip to Ackerman. Whether the old reporter was a part of the threat or merely being used as a pawn based on his explainable proximity to the exhibit, her potential lack of discretion was still a problem.

Given Mia's mulish expression, that was an opinion he was going to keep to himself.

Finished eating, she set her fork aside. "Listen, Tanner. I know you're doing your job, but I trust my people. And as far as the rest of the staff is concerned, the dummy statue is the real McCoy. They're transporting it with as much care as they've always done."

That still didn't explain why Ackerman had come to her apartment. Why he'd been so determined to follow *her*. Was the man really that intuitive, or had he been tipped off in some capacity?

"Then why did Ackerman want to follow you?" he asked, voicing his thoughts. "By your reasoning, he should be following the exhibit."

She paled. "I hadn't thought of that."

Tanner felt his muscles clench. He should have thought of it much sooner. And there was something else he should have thought of, as well, he realized as the back of his neck prickled with that same sense of uneasiness he'd been feeling all damned morning.

He swore. "Time to resume our happy lovers role," he announced as he tossed some cash onto the table.

Her eyes widened. "What? Why?"

He slid out of the booth, grabbing the backpack in the process, then offered Mia his hand. He leaned in and pressed a kiss to her cheek, felt the touch sizzle to the soles of his feet. "Because I'm 99.9 percent certain that we're being watched. And I'm even more certain that there's a GPS device somewhere under the car."

MIA GASPED. A GPS device under the car? How? When? *What the hell?* Her mind whirling, Tanner slung an arm over her shoulder and herded her through the small lobby of the hotel. From the corner of her eye, she watched him covertly scan the room. Tension and irritation vibrated off his powerful frame, making her acutely aware of his sudden displeasure. He leaned over, smiled as though imparting a private thought and whispered into her ear. "Wait until we get into the car before you start firing questions at me, okay, Bossy? I know it's killing you, but you'll make it. Now giggle flirtatiously and grab my ass."

He said it with such authority that her first reaction was to obey. She'd actually dropped her palm and was on the verge of doing exactly what she'd been told until what he'd said fully registered. She fisted her hand instead and mentally cursed herself.

She smiled up at him and batted her lashes. "Rot in hell."

The wretch actually grinned, then shrugged. "It was worth a shot."

"You're insufferable."

"I think you're a wonderful lover, too," Tanner said in a tone that carried, much to her mortification. "You rocked my world so hard last night, I think I'm going to have to nickname you The Quake." He opened the car door for her and she felt his gaze slide over her breasts. Her thighs, damn them, quivered.

Mia snorted. "And I suppose I should nickname you The Noodle because of your limp—"

His expression gratifyingly horrified, he gave her a gentle shove, toppling her into the car. Then he shut the door before she could finish.

Mia was shaking with silent laughter when he slid behind the wheel. "Sorry," she said, the apology automatic.

"No, you're not, you liar. You're quite pleased with yourself." He took stock of the parking lot, adjusted the mirrors, then backed away from the curb and aimed the car toward the exit.

She was pleased with herself, actually, so she didn't bother trying to deny it. "The Quake," she repeated with a derisive snort. "You make me sound like a member of the World Wrestling Federation."

His smile was so lazy it was evil. "I wouldn't mind watching you roll around in the mud. Or in a pool of Jell-O. Naked."

She felt her lips twitch and found herself reluctantly flattered. "I'd forgotten how shallow you were."

"Don't worry. I'm going to remind you, every opportunity I get."

"Something to look forward to then," she remarked drolly. "Goody." She snagged her sunglasses from her bag, then slid them onto her nose. "I can't decide if you're really this easily distracted or if you're purposely toying with me so that I won't ask you about the whole being watched/GPS issue."

He continued to watch the mirrors, presumably looking for whoever was following them. "How do you know I'm not doing both?"

"You've learned to multitask? Excellent. It's a valuable life skill."

He directed a long-suffering glare at her but didn't comment. "Ackerman was in the parking lot when we came down from the apartment. If he followed us from the museum, then he had ample time to plant the device."

"But he thought we were going to the airport. How could he have known that I'd be going with you?"

Tanner shrugged. "Hedging his bets. Bottom line, he knew where you were staying when he shouldn't have, he was there and he had the opportunity. Duck Theory 101."

She frowned. "Duck Theory 101? I don't think I'm familiar with that particular class."

"If it walks like a duck, talks like a duck—"

"Then it's a duck," she finished for him. Though her

instinctive response was to argue with him, Mia found that she couldn't. Tanner's "theory" made as much sense as anything else did. "How do you know we're being watched?"

His gaze covertly slid to the rearview mirror again. "I didn't know for sure until about thirty seconds ago. But the hair on the back of my neck has been standing up since we walked into the restaurant this morning. I could feel it, even if I couldn't see it."

She hadn't noticed it at all and she briefly wondered if that meant her antennae were broken or if Tanner's considerable sex appeal was scrambling the signal. Her money was on the latter. "But you see it now?"

He nodded. "Pretend to be checking your makeup in the visor. Five cars back, left-hand lane. White minivan. Does the person driving look familiar?"

Mia did as he instructed, touching up her lip gloss in the process. "It's Ackerman's woman," she said, then frowned. "I don't remember them being in a minivan."

"Ackerman only let me think I'd shaken him. Once he'd planted the device and knew we weren't going to the airport, he swapped rentals and caught up with us."

Mia bit her bottom lip, her stomach getting queasy. "I wouldn't have thought he was that smart," she said.

"He's an investigative reporter," Tanner told her. "I don't know that he's so much smart, as sneaky."

Mia swallowed and her gaze drifted to the backpack stowed at her feet and thought of the priceless antiquity it housed, the one she was charged with helping to keep safe. More than her job was on the line here—a piece of history was, as well. Knowing that the threat was possible was one thing—actually having someone follow them was quite another.

Though she'd always thought Ackerman's interest was a little too keen, she'd never felt threatened by him. She'd never been afraid of him. Had she been wrong? Mia wondered now. Could he be working for Ramirez?

As a journalist, he had a valid reason for following the exhibit, supposedly reporting on the "fertility phenomenon." He was the perfect plant, the kind who wouldn't raise a lot of suspicion. She shared her thoughts with Tanner.

"To tell you the truth, I just always thought he was a little strange, that he'd decided this story was going to be the one that got him the recognition he deserved," she told him. "I never would have put him in league with Ramirez. But considering the lengths he's going to now…I don't know."

"I don't, either," Tanner said. "But the only way he's getting his hands on Moe Dick is by coming through me—" he chuckled darkly "—and I can assure you, sweetheart, I'm not going to let that happen. This is my first assignment for Ranger Security and I'll be damned before I let a second-rate reporter or a wealthy thug screw it up." There was a strange undercurrent in his voice that she didn't readily identify. Desperation, maybe?

Honestly, when he'd been so quiet at breakfast this morning, she'd chalked it up to humiliation from last night. When he'd given her the reluctant so-nonchalant-it-was-painful warning about his possible nightmares, she'd had no idea what to expect. A whimper maybe, a little thrashing beneath the covers.

No.

"Not the school, damn you! Not the school, you miserable bastards! No, dammit, no! God, no!"

He'd screamed like he was dying and then moaned like he wished he had.

It was utterly heartbreaking.

The first shout had woken her from a dead sleep—one that had taken forever to reach due to his damned distracting, half-naked proximity—and she'd needed to use more than a sharp jab to wake him from the awful dream. She'd had to grab his shoulders and shake him, repeatedly saying his name until she got his attention. He'd been clammy with sweat, breathing hard and the shame that passed over his gaze as soon as he realized that she'd witnessed his terror was quite possibly the saddest thing she'd ever seen.

But it clearly wasn't the saddest thing *he'd* ever seen.

He'd apologized, lumbered to the bathroom where she'd heard him retch, then washed his mouth out and returned to their room. She'd purposely turned her back to the bathroom door, trying not to humiliate him by witnessing anymore of his pain. She'd felt his gaze linger on her for a moment before he finally slid back into his bed.

What had happened to him? Mia wondered. What

horror haunted him to the point that he'd left the military? She had her suspicions, of course, given his agonized outburst about the school and the mere thought was too horrible to imagine. How cowardly that she didn't even want to imagine what he'd been forced to witness.

Her gaze slid to Tanner, who was carefully negotiating traffic. Fatigue tightened the skin around his eyes and his usually smiling mouth was grim with determination. His thick tawny locks were slowing growing out of the military cut, reminding her more of the boy she once new. Her heart gave a little pang and she resisted the urge to reach over and stroke his cheek. Mia heaved a small sigh.

It was so much easier to deal with him when he was being a smart-ass.

"At the restaurant, when you looked out the window and frowned," he prompted. "What did you see?"

It took her brain a second to switch gears. "Nothing," she said, instantly tense. "My eyes were playing tricks on me."

"What did your tricky eyes think they saw, then?" Tanner pressed. "Everything is significant, Mia. Even if you don't think it is."

She genuinely didn't want to discuss this with him. Her father was a sore subject, a sad and disgraceful one she preferred to keep private. All she'd ever told Tanner about her dad was that he'd exited her life when she was ten. She hadn't told him about his diverse criminal records, his general lack of regard for anyone around him, his pathological lying and textbook narcissistic behavior. It was humiliating and made her feel like she had bad blood.

But, ultimately, he was right. Everything was significant. She looked out the window, watched the bright green landscape roll by as they sped down eighty-one south toward Knoxville. Mia had actually plotted their route before they'd left and was secretly pleased to see that Tanner was unknowingly following the same course she'd plotted. She heaved a small sigh, dragged her knitting needles and yarn from her bag and set to work.

"I thought I saw my father," she finally admitted. "In a car that came through the parking lot."

Tanner's brow creased. "Your father? Wouldn't you have known if it was him?"

A valid question, one she didn't want to answer. She corrected a dropped stitch and knitted faster. "In a perfect world, yes," she admitted. "In reality, however, I haven't seen my dad in three years. And, to tell you the truth, hadn't seen him several years before that."

"That's right," Tanner murmured, still watching the rearview mirror. "He left when you were young." He shot her an apologetic look. "Sorry, Mia. I should have remembered," he said, his voice laced with regret.

She shook her head, dismissing his apology. "It was just bizarre. He's tried to contact me a couple of times in the past few weeks, but I just assumed I was his one phone call and he was between women of questionable intelligence." If she sounded bitter, it's because she was.

Tanner didn't so much as bat a lash, but she recognized a sudden change all the same. "He's done time?"

"Not for more than a few months at a stretch, I think." Mia finished off the sock, adding her trademark linked initials in white on the upper hem. She did them in lowercase, so they looked a bit like a pitchfork.

Tanner glanced over, seemingly distracted for a moment by what she was doing. He'd watched her knit yesterday afternoon and last night, as well, but she'd been working on a cap then. "Who are those for?" he asked, his voice strange.

Mia retrieved the other sock from her bag and folded them together, then put them into a plastic bag. "I don't know specifically," she admitted. "I belong to a knitting group who makes socks and caps and the like for soldiers stationed overseas. I've been doing it for years." It seemed like the least that she could do for the men and women serving their country. The whole idea had struck a deep chord within her and she'd enjoyed being able to contribute, even it was with something as small as a pair of socks.

A disbelieving smile slid over his lips and he shook his head. "I've got a pair of those," he told her. "And, as improbable as this sounds, I swear, I think they're a pair of yours. They've got the same little pitchfork on the top, just like that, only they're a different color. Either gray or light blue."

Unreasonably pleased, Mia smiled. "That's not a pitchfork, fool. It's my initials—MH."

He smiled as understanding dawned. "Ah." He sighed. "Now I see. Very clever."

She thought so, but she was biased, Mia thought, starting another pair.

"Back to your father," he said. "What had he been put away for? Do you know?"

"Petty theft. Running scams on the elderly. Stealing checks, bad checks, basically anything that's dishonorable and stupid."

Tanner seemed to be mulling that over. "Would Ramirez be the kind of man your father could be involved with?"

Mia was suddenly sick to her stomach. "Honestly, Tanner, I don't know. I can't imagine that's the case— Ramirez is way out of my father's league—but with my father and what little I know of him, I guess anything is possible."

And sadly, that was the truth. Furthermore, if she found out her father was behind any of this, she'd personally throttle him. He'd already mucked up her childhood—she'd be damned before she allowed him to interfere with the career she was building.

"So what are we going to do about the tracking device?" she finally asked, deciding that a subject change was in order.

"Don't worry," he told her. "I've got a plan."

She felt her lips twitch. "Let me guess. This plan will at some point, involve you telling me to follow your lead?"

He laughed, checked the rearview mirror, then hit

the accelerator and darted across three lanes to the exit at the last possible second, leaving the minivan behind on the interstate.

"Of course. It's one of my more inspired plans."

She rolled her eyes. "I'm beginning to think it's your *only* plan."

And fool that she was, she actually liked it.

7

TANNER QUICKLY PULLED into a truck stop and drove to the back of the lot, where the cache of eighteen-wheelers would give them a decent bit of cover.

"We need to get another rental."

Without further explanation on his part, Mia pulled out her phone. "I'm on it."

A thought struck. "Here," he said, tossing her his cell. "Use mine."

She frowned, but wonder of wonders, she didn't argue.

Tanner locked her inside with their precious cargo, then dropped to his knees and began feeling around underneath the car. He hit pay dirt behind the right back passenger tire, tucked high in the wheel well. The bumpers wouldn't have worked—too much plastic.

With a grim smile, he tapped on the window, showed the device to Mia, then turned and stuck it underneath a nearby transfer truck. With any luck, this guy would roll out in a few minutes and lay a false trail. In the interim, a new car and a different route away from the interstate was going to be in order. It would slow them down for a bit, but they should still make Nashville this evening as planned. A droll smile touched his lips.

Contrary to what Mia thought, he *did* have a plan. It was just more fun to leave her in the dark about it.

But leaving her *alone* in the dark was a completely different matter, particularly when he could hear the soft breath breezing between her lips, the slide of her hair over the pillow, soft murmurs in her sleep. And that little nightie thing she'd been wearing? What in sweet hell had he ever done to deserve that sort of torment?

Obviously she hadn't realized she was going to be sharing a room with her security agent. Otherwise he was certain she would have packed something that covered more of her body than the silky scrap of pale pink fabric and lace he'd gotten a peek of last night when she'd shimmied quickly out of her robe and launched herself beneath the covers. It had reminded him of those old vaudeville shows where the virgin heroine had cowered under the covers while the evil villain menacingly stroked his mustache.

As if he hadn't seen it all before.

He'd chuckled and she'd glared. Good times.

Furthermore, though she'd always held a special attraction for him, something about seeing her again had made him unbelievably hyper-aware of her. The shape of her mouth, the ripeness of her breasts, the lush curve of her hip and her ass… Damn, how he wanted to get his hands on it, to feel it beneath his palms. He was constantly, hammeringly aware of her, could practically feel her in his blood…and most of that was pooled south of his brain.

Logic told him it was natural, that it was just a by-product of a.) not being laid recently and b.) being with an extremely sexy woman with whom he shared a spectacularly carnal past. But if he'd had a dollar for every time his gaze had slid to the backpack and imagined the little statue contained within…

Impossible.

Tanner was familiar with being horny. He'd been tapping cheerleaders since junior high—the sight of a pair of pom-poms still gave him a little thrill—and he'd furthered his sexual expertise during his teenage years courtesy of a friend's father's extensive porn library. What could he say? Tanner thought with a grin. He was a visual learner.

At any rate, he'd been everything from mildly horny to desperately-in-need-of-an-orgasm and yet the level of lust which was currently plaguing him was an altogether new experience. He didn't believe for a minute that it had anything to do with Moe Dick—no matter how often his gaze was drawn to the backpack—and had found himself shocked to learn that Mia did. How bizarre that someone so sensible could buy into what was obviously brought about by the mighty power of suggestion.

As if this wrestling with the all-consuming attraction wasn't enough, he had to deal with the knowledge that she'd witnessed one of his mortifying nightmares. Considering he hadn't had a single night since the incident without one, he knew it was inevitable. But having her see it? *Damn*. His cheeks burned with remembered humiliation.

And this had been a particularly bad one, one that brought up an image he hadn't realized had been stored in his head. *So much death. So many little bodies.* He squeezed his eyes tightly shut, forcing the images back. He'd actually been so shaken up, he'd been sick to his stomach. She had to have heard that, too, and yet thankfully—blessedly—when he'd returned to the bedroom, she'd turned away from the door, giving him a bit of privacy. Not many women would have been so intuitive, would have known that he'd needed that small reprieve. But she had and, as further testament to her character, she hadn't asked the first question.

Tanner slid back into the car and turned to look at her. "Where are we going?"

She quickly rattled off directions and he aimed the sedan in the appropriate direction. "They've only got one car left," she said, a curious note of humor in her voice that put him instantly on guard.

"Oh?"

"I told them to hold it. At this point, I don't think we can a-afford to be p-picky." She clamped her lips together, presumably to keep from smiling.

Dread ballooned in his gut. "What is it?"

She fiddled with the end of her braid. "Oh, you'll see."

And he did, a moment later. His eyes widened and he

swore hotly. "A Smart car? Seriously? That's all they've got left?"

"Yes." And then she howled with laughter.

Tanner offered a friendly wave to the staff as he wheeled through the parking lot, then shot back out into traffic. "We'll find another one."

Her mouth fell open. "What? Are you serious? I knew you wouldn't like it, but I didn't think you'd be such a snob."

"It's not a matter of being a snob, it's a matter of being comfortable. I am six-six. You are what? Five-two, Five-three?"

"I'm five-five actually," she said primly, tilting her adorable nose up into the air.

"Bullshit. Maybe in those god-awful heels." He spied a Chevrolet dealership ahead on the right and prayed they'd have a rental department. "The point is, I don't intend to spend the next eighteen to twenty hours with my knees up to my ears just because *you* think it's funny."

"That may be true, but you wouldn't be caught dead in a Smart car even if you only had to drive it across the street. Its small size impugns your masculinity."

Tanner chuckled under his breath and slid her a look. "There is very damned little that impugns my masculinity."

Something shifted in her gaze, melted. She swallowed. "That secure, are you?"

He nodded once. "Damn straight."

"So how many gay friends do you have?"

"Two," he answered truthfully. Ruthie and Marge

were a wonderful couple, two of the nicest lesbians anyone could ever meet. And he suspected the office manager at Ranger Security didn't bat for his team, either, but he seemed like a fine enough fellow. To each his own, was Tanner's motto. It didn't make him any less hetero.

Seemingly stumped, she hummed under her breath. "So what kind of car are you going to get?"

"One with ample legroom." His gaze slid over her short, curvy frame and a bolt of heat landed in his groin. "That's something a midget like you doesn't have to worry about."

"I don't mind being short," she said, eyeing the new model cars as they pulled through the lot to the rental department.

He laughed and quirked a sardonic brow. "So you wear the heels because they're so comfortable?" he drawled.

She rolled her head toward him and gave him a smile that put him in mind of crisp white sheets, hot oil and a rainy afternoon. "I wear them because they make me feel sexy."

His tongue suddenly felt too thick for his mouth and he struggled to swallow. "That's a good enough reason, I suppose."

He mentally stripped her down to the heels, then redressed her in the little gown she had on last night. *Creamy thighs, mouthwatering cleavage, the hint of a pearled nipple behind satin.*

He went hard.

She grinned and arched a knowing brow. "Do you need a minute?"

She was evil. Purely, utterly evil.

Pity he found that so damned attractive.

He cupped the back of her neck with his hand and drew her forward, then hungrily attached his mouth to hers. She tasted like maple syrup and coffee, like cool rain after too many years in the desert, like anticipation and redemption. A low moan signaled her surrender— the sweetest thing he'd tasted so far—and she tunneled her fingers into his hair and pressed herself against him.

His entire body vibrated with need as her tongue tangled around his, an unspeakably wonderful seek and retreat that he wanted to mimic with another body part below his waist, one that was in serious danger of popping above of the waistband of his jeans. He was breathing her in, absorbing her essence, savoring the feel of her against his mouth. Her lips were full and sensual, the upper a little plumper on one side, which gave the impression that she was always enjoying a private joke. A provocative imperfection he'd once heard her lament, but he adored it.

Breathing heavily, she tore her mouth from his. "Who's watching?" she gasped brokenly.

"The salespeople, I imagine." He nuzzled her cheek with his nose. He could smell her lotion, something fruity and sweet. God, he could just eat her up. She was luscious. Perfect.

She blinked drunkenly up at him, then her muddled

gaze turned into a glare. "B-but I was following your lead."

He chewed the inside of his cheek. "Yes, you were. Without direction and quite brilliantly, I might add. I'm so proud of you."

With a disgusted grunt, she shoved hard at his chest. "Idiot," she growled. "You scared me half to death. I was afraid they'd somehow found us again already."

His gaze dropped to her mouth and he lowered his voice. "I'm glad I was able to take your mind off it for a minute."

Her eyes narrowed. "You're a real piece of work, Tanner, you know that?"

"Yes." He wraggled his brows. "A *master*piece."

"I was thinking more along the lines of a piece of—"

"Hey," he interrupted, feigning a wounded look. "No need for name-calling. You shouldn't be so hard on yourself."

Her eyes widened. "On myself? You're the one I'm angry with!"

"Possibly. But not all of that anger's for me." He studied her thoughtfully for a moment and it unnerved her to the point she looked away. A deep blush stained her cheeks. "I think you're mad at yourself because you enjoyed it a whole lot more than you wanted to."

And with that parting comment, he snagged the backpack and climbed from the car. While she was fuming, he put in a quick call to Ranger Security. He needed a little more information on Mia's erstwhile sire and he didn't want to humiliate her by making her listen to him while he asked for it.

Bastard, Tanner thought. If he was behind any part of this, Tanner fully intended to give the man a thrashing he wouldn't forget. He'd seen the tightness appear around her mouth when he'd asked if her father would consort with Ramirez, the shame in her eyes as she'd unwillingly shared the kind of person he was. Her father had hurt her and for that reason alone, he'd like to kick his ass.

Somebody needed to for what the man had done to his daughter, that was for damned sure. And Tanner was more than happy to do the job.

THE DAMNED KNOW-IT-ALL, Mia thought, as she waited for her personal mercury to cool. She hadn't remembered him being so perceptive. Was it an acquired skill? she wondered, or had she just been too much in love with him to notice the last time around?

Though she thought her acting skills were improving, she knew they wouldn't carry her so far as to pretend that his kiss—hell, simply being around him—wasn't affecting her.

It was.

Oh, how it was.

Her toes had been curling to the point she'd almost developed cramps and the hot zing of need pinging in her womb to the tune of what she suspected was his heartbeat was making her squirm in her seat like a grounded toddler forced to sit in the naughty chair. She didn't know what sort of cologne he was wearing, but it was absolutely *driving her crazy.* It made her want to suck him up like a Slurpee. Her breasts ached behind her bra and the hot, muddled sensation camping low in her belly seemed to intensify with every agitated breath.

And looking at him only made things worse. The shape of those full, sculpted lips, the lean slope of his cheek, the firm edge of his jaw and even the side of his neck—a place she'd love to lean over and kiss just below his ear—taunted her with every glimpse.

And when he looked at her dead-on? Despite repeated exposure, she was never quite prepared for the combination of need and reluctant, bittersweet affection that slammed into her. It left her breathless and light-headed. The desire she could justify. Between his naturally potent sexual appeal and Moe exerting his significant influence, it was no wonder that she found herself locked in a state of practically debilitating lust.

But those softer emotions? The ones that made her heart give a pathetic little jump, her resolve melt, her lips curl of their own volition...those, she knew, were trouble.

Tanner snapped his phone shut and rounded the hood, then opened her door. She hadn't been waiting on him to do it—she just hadn't gathered her wits about her enough to exit on her own power. While other women might object to such an old-fashioned gesture, Mia had to admit that she wasn't one of them. She appreciated the courtesy and took it as a sign of respect rather than an insult to her gender.

In relatively short order, he'd arranged to have the other car returned to the proper rental company and procured a replacement, a crossover SUV with enough legroom for comfort and pickup speed to disappear quickly if needed. She'd listened as he'd made the call to Ranger Security and briefed them on the changes to their situation and found herself reluctantly impressed with his performance.

Not that she shouldn't have been. Tanner had always been more than competent. He had a keen brain behind all that masculine beauty and brawn, and a dedication of purpose that had surpassed so many of their contemporaries. It had been part of what had drawn her to him from the start. She'd appreciated his drive, his ambition, his desire to not just inhabit the world in which he lived, but to try and better it. It was an admirable quality, one of many.

"Okay," Tanner said, as slipped his phone back into the holder at his waist. "New plan. I know that the original arrangement involved keeping your PA and head of security in the loop, but in light of Ackerman's obvious involvement and resulting breach, we're not going to do that."

Mia absorbed that. "You don't want me to check in?"

"Yes, I do. We need to keep up with any new developments on their end, but I don't want you to disclose our location. We're going to pick up a few disposable phones so that you can contact them. But if they need to contact you, then whatever information they need to share will be routed through Ranger Security directly to me."

Her head whirled. "Why?"

"Because if Ackerman knew where you were staying, then it's possible that he has your cell-phone number. And if he's in bed with Ramirez, then Ramirez has the resources to trace your whereabouts through the phone. Have you made or taken any calls?"

"No," Mia said, shaken. Well, that explained why he'd wanted her to use his phone instead of hers to find the rental agency.

"Good," Tanner said with a nod. "Turn it off."

Feeling strangely numb, she did.

Tanner started to say something, then hesitated a moment. "Listen, if you'll give me the numbers, I can call the office and have them forward your temporary emergency contact information to anyone you would want to have it."

She looked up and blinked, not following.

He released a small sigh. "Like Harlan," he said, the words seemingly pulled out of him. "Or your mother."

A little pinch of pain squeezed her heart at the casual reference to her mom. "I won't hear from Harlan," she said. No doubt her efficient ex had already packed up whatever belongings she had at his apartment and forwarded them to Savannah. She had to clear her throat. "And I, um… I lost my mother three years ago. Ovarian cancer."

She watched the shock register on his face. He winced

with regret and reached over to grab her hand. "I'm so sorry, Mia. I remember you were very close to her."

Her mom had been her best friend and her rock, her faithful cheerleader and her confidante. While she'd had several friends whose mothers drove them insane, Mia had never been able to relate to their relationships. Though her mother had never remarried, being Mia's mother hadn't become the thing that defined her. Jane Hawthorne had had lots of interests, a host of friends and a busy career that begged for her time and she'd balanced them beautifully. Mia had always known that she came first, but without the guilt or resentment brought about by the divorce. Her mother had been a strong woman, a force of nature and the world was most definitely a much bleaker place without her in it.

"Thank you," she said, for lack of anything better. "I miss her."

He squeezed her hand again, but to her pleasure, he didn't release it. A shadow suddenly moved behind his eyes and she watched a weariness settle along his jaw. "Death's a bitch."

He'd certainly seen his share of that, Mia knew and something about the grim tone of his voice made her ache for him. Between the nature of his career and the nightmare she'd witnessed last night, she knew Tanner was carrying around his own grief demons, as well. There was a brief instance of perfect understanding between them in that moment and, for whatever reason, it united them in a present that lacked the clutter of the past.

To her chagrin, the thought was as comforting as it was terrifying.

8

IT WAS AMAZING HOW easily information could be bought, the man thought, smiling, even when that knowledge shouldn't be sold. Thanks to his informant, he knew that Mia and her mystery man had stopped at a chain motel outside Roanoke. He knew that they'd shared a room and ordered dinner from the place next door. He knew that the man had eaten a sizable breakfast and had ordered coffee. Mia had opted for a simple bagel and hot tea.

Interestingly, the backpack had never left the man's possession.

And even more noteworthy, the corporate card he'd used to pay for the room was registered to Ranger Security.

The man chuckled softly, and picked up the phone. His goal was finally—thrillingly—within reach. And he'd stop at nothing to achieve it.

Absolutely nothing.

"SOPHIE'S HURT," MIA said later, frowning down at one of the new cell phones they'd picked up just before they'd stopped for lunch. "She thinks I don't trust her."

Tanner dredged a fry through a pool of ketchup and enjoyed the feel of the sun on his back. They'd chosen a fast-food restaurant for expediency's sake and had opted to sit outside in the fenced-in play area for children so that they could keep a close eye on the parking lot.

Though he thought they were safe, he intended to be much more careful from here on out. They'd abandoned the interstate for a less-predictable route and hoped that the tracking device he'd transferred to the truck would lead their pursuers in the wrong direction for a while, buying them some time to get a decent head start.

"It's not a matter of trust, Mia, it's a matter of precaution," he explained. "The less anyone knows, the better we are. We're eliminating room for error. If we're compromised again, it'll be easier to narrow down the source."

She picked glumly at her salad. "I understand the logic, Tanner, I just wish it wasn't necessary."

"Being with me is that terrible, is it?" he teased, pretending like her answer didn't matter.

She smiled and shot him a look, but to his irrational displeasure, she completely ignored the question. "She did confirm that Ackerman and his companion spent a lot of time hanging out at the hotel where the staff was based in D.C. So it's possible that he noticed I wasn't there and decided to follow me to Harlan's apartment."

It was just as possible that someone let something slip—Tanner thought the man was a reporter, after all, and prying was his business—but he wasn't going to argue the point with her. He watched a couple of kids climb through the netting overhead, enjoying their laughter. "The exhibit was in Atlanta prior to D.C., correct?"

Mia nodded.

"And did you stay in the same hotel as the rest of the staff then?"

"I did."

"I'm assuming Ackerman was making a nuisance of himself there, as well?"

Her gaze turned thoughtful. "He was…though he was alone then," she added as an afterthought. Something niggled in her brain, but disappeared before she could decipher the meaning behind it.

"So he would have noticed when you weren't around in D.C." He shrugged. "Your absence from the group would have invited his curiosity at the very least."

"I suppose," she admitted with a sigh. "I'll just be glad when we get to Dallas and this becomes someone else's problem."

"It already is," he pointed out. *"Mine."*

She had the grace to blush. She looked up and winced. "Sorry," she said, chagrined. "I didn't mean that the way that it sounded. You're doing a great job."

Pride bloomed in his chest at her casual praise and he laughed softly. "That's debatable, but I intend to do better."

"Do you think you're going to enjoy this line of work then?"

Finished eating, Tanner wadded his napkin and tossed it on his tray. He considered her question and wondered how he could answer without making her feel like he was prevaricating. He didn't want to talk about this. He didn't want to tell her about his former job and how he'd failed. He didn't want to think about what had happened, let alone share any of it with her. It was too hard, too painful, too shameful.

You're a disgrace. Weak. I'm ashamed of you.

"I think so," he said. "New assignments, new circumstances." He took a swallow from his drink and suddenly wished it was something stronger. "No opportunity for things to get stale."

She studied him for a minute in that thoughtful way she had, those warm brown eyes searching his. Though he knew it was impossible, he could practically feel her plucking the truth out of his head, spotting the lies, separating fact from fiction like wheat from the chaff.

But it was better for her to think he'd gotten bored, than gotten soft. That he'd blown it.

The mere idea was unthinkable.

Just when he was convinced she was going to ask if that's what happened, that he'd gotten tired of the military, she pulled in a deep breath and smiled at him. "That's the thing about history—even though it's old, I'm always finding something new."

Relief made his cramped fingers go limp. He released

a breath he hadn't realized he'd been holding. "So you're happy then?"

"With my job?" She nodded once. "Definitely. I love working with the Center. All in all, I've got it made. I've got the freedom to broaden my studies when the urge strikes and have earned the confidence of the administrators to work with different projects and exhibits that interest me."

He jerked his head toward the backpack. "Like Moe Dick?"

She chuckled and bit her bottom lip. "Laugh all you want, but…yes. Like anything else, sex has its own evolving history and the ancient cultures were just as fascinated with it as their modern-day counterparts." She sent him a pointed look. "But the one constant, the thing that never changes, is the desire to populate the earth, to bring forth the next generation." Her gaze slid to the backpack. "That's Moe's ultimate purpose. You look at him and see something lewd. I look at him and see another civilization who wanted to thrive. And he's still relevant today. If he wasn't, we wouldn't be on this adventure."

He shot her a skeptical glance. "So you really believe that he works?"

She nodded. "I've felt the…effects myself."

"The effects?"

She looked away and her lips curled into a slightly embarrassed smile. "Yes, the effects," she said significantly.

Tanner leaned forward. "I'm afraid I'm not following,"

he lied. He knew perfectly well what she was talking about. He just liked to see her squirm. It could easily become his favorite source of entertainment.

"In order to procreate, one must be in the mood," she explained, blushing to her hairline, where her eyebrows suddenly disappeared.

"Ah." He sighed knowingly. "And you've been in the mood?"

"Excruciatingly so, for the past six weeks." She rubbed the bridge of her nose and shook her head. A bark of laughter erupted from her throat. "I can't believe I'm telling *you,* of all people, *this.* But yes, a thousand times yes. And I'm not the only one. Just look at what's been happening to the people looking after the exhibit. Staff who are married have been bringing their spouses along to take the edge off. And the single ones have been hooking up like sailors on a three-day pass. It's been *unreal.* We've got three girls on staff who are pregnant already."

"And you think this is Moe's fault?"

She shrugged fatalistically. "The evidence speaks for itself. Are you telling me that you're immune? That you haven't had sex on the brain since you've been around Moe?"

"Not because of Moe," he said, his gaze lingering hungrily on her mouth. He studied her again, the idea of her being excruciatingly horny reverberating in his brain like a pistol shot. His dick stirred in his jeans and he let his gaze drop to her mouth once more.

He smiled and chewed the inside of his cheek. "Bad time for you to break up with your boyfriend, huh?"

She laughed weakly and her keen gaze tangled with his. "I'll manage."

He gave her a confident nod and grinned. "Let me know if you need any help. I can hook you up."

Stupid, stupid, stupid. This was wrong on so many levels he didn't even know where to start. In the first place, he was technically working, although considering one of his bosses had tossed him a *box of condoms,* for crying out loud, before he left, he didn't think they'd fire him over it. In the second place, this was Mia, the only girl he'd ever been emotionally invested in. Leaving her the first time had been like lopping off an appendage, but he'd had his ambition to distract him, so he'd filled the void with adrenaline and casual sex.

He'd survived.

Something told him he wouldn't this time.

And lastly...he was a mess. It was hard enough to inhabit his own skin much less invite someone else in.

But *damn* how he wanted her—how he burned and ached to have her—and he didn't believe for a minute that it had anything whatsoever to do with Moe. There had always been something about Mia that had simply lit him up. She was the perfect combination of funny and smart, sexy and wholesome.

From the first moment he'd met her all those years ago, he'd recognized that there was something special— something singularly unique—about *her.* She'd made him feel differently, had made him want to be more, to be better.

"So where are we headed now?" she asked, thankfully pulling him out of his reverie.

"To Nashville," he said. "And just in the nick of time, too," he told her, nodding toward a little boy standing near the slide who was holding himself. "There's obviously a wienie thief in the area and since we're carrying a big one, we'd better get going."

Her eyes widened and she choked on the drink she'd been taking. "A wienie thief?" she asked, following his gaze. She gasped and a laugh bubbled up her throat. "You're horrible, Tanner," she admonished with a smile.

He stood and shrugged. "I'm just considering the evidence. And the way that kid is holding on to his little—"

"Yeah, yeah," she said, cutting him off. She snorted and whacked him on the arm. "A wienie thief." She looked heavenward, as though seeking divine assistance. "What am I going to do with you?"

He put his hand in the small of her back and, gratifyingly, felt her shiver. Heat buzzed up his arm and pooled in his groin. "Am I allowed to make a suggestion?" he murmured hopefully.

"No."

"Damn." He winced with regret. "I think you would have liked it."

She groaned and muttered something that sounded suspiciously like, "That's exactly what I'm afraid of."

He chuckled. "I'm sorry, what was that?"

"Nothing."

Liar.

MIA HAD MADE MANY stupid mistakes over the years—attempting to boil an egg in the microwave (it exploded), closing her own hair in the car door (while not impossible, it was quite painful), mixing ammonia and bleach while cleaning the kitchen sink (she almost passed out)—but confiding her extremely horny condition to Tanner had to take first freakin' prize.

From the moment they'd gotten back into the car, he'd been purposely trying to drive her crazy. Crowding into her personal space, touching her unnecessarily, shooting her those heavy-lidded looks. And that wicked smile...

She shivered, remembering.

She'd hoped that once they'd reached Nashville and settled into their room, she might get a reprieve, but he'd asked for the shower first and, to her mixed delight and horror, had accidentally, on purpose, failed to completely close the bathroom door. She'd gotten a prime view of his back as he'd pulled his shirt up over his head, and the muscle play across his shoulders had been nothing short of mouthwatering.

And when he'd shucked his jeans...

Mia inhaled sharply. *Fluted spine, lean waist, perfectly proportioned ass.* She'd caught a glimpse of the rest of him when he'd turned to walk toward the shower and that fleeting look was more than enough to make the top of her thighs catch on fire.

His ass wasn't the only thing that was well-proportioned.

Her gaze slid to Moe, where he rested in the back-pack and she could have sworn she saw the air shimmer around it. She squeezed her eyes tightly shut and struggled to find focus.

Steam was slowly billowing through the bathroom door and the scent of Tanner's soap—sandalwood, maybe?—was creeping into the room, further intoxicating her already sluggish system. It took very little imagination to picture soapy water sluicing over those magnificent muscles, clinging to the hair on his chest and following the treasure trail that bisected his stomach and disappeared below his waist.

Mia squeezed her eyes tightly shut and swore. A distraction, that's what she needed, she thought, fisting her hands in her hair and giving a little tug to clear her mind. Her gaze cast about the room for something to do and landed on the remote control. She snatched it up in favor of knitting—she didn't trust sharp objects in her hands at the moment—and aimed it at the television. Her iPod was charging, otherwise some Monty Python would be just the ticket.

In some miserable, cosmic twist of fate a commercial for his and hers KY Gel instantly filled the screen.

She groaned and quickly changed the channel. Ah, the weather. That should be safe, right?

"Get ready, folks," the anchorman said as a giant sun

suddenly glowed hugely behind him. "It's going to be hot, hot, hot over the next several days."

No shit, Sherlock, Mia thought, a hysterical laugh erupting from her throat. She clicked the remote again and breathed an audible sigh of relief when she landed on a familiar sitcom.

"Something wrong?" Tanner asked as he strolled out of the bathroom, the towel resting precariously on his lean hips. The edge of the tattoo she'd noted beneath his T-shirt was fully visible now and she smiled when she saw it. A raven resting on a branch, painted in stark black ink on his biceps. A nod to Poe, she thought, deeming it fitting. He sauntered over to his bag and withdrew a pair of boxers.

Her mouth went dry. Supple muscle, sleek skin, mile-wide shoulders, abs that were so well-defined they made the traditional six-pack look shabby. Water clung to his tawny locks and beaded over his back, and his nose and the tops of his ears gleamed in the lamplight.

Without warning, he dropped the towel and stepped into his shorts.

She groaned and glared at the ceiling. "Do you mind, Tanner? I'm right here."

He turned and grinned at her, the wretch. "Sorry," he said, though he didn't sound sorry at all. His eyes twinkled. "Modesty is one of the first things you lose in a locker room."

"We're not in a locker room."

His unbelievably carnal mouth twitched. "Believe it or not, I'd worked that one out for myself."

He'd reduced her to pointing out the obvious. Sheesh. Mia popped up from the bed. "I think I'll go ahead and have a shower, as well."

"I'd wait a minute," he said. "Give the water time to heat up."

She gathered her toiletries. "I'll take my chances."

His chuckle followed her into the bathroom, where she sagged against the countertop and stared at her foggy reflection. "You've got to get a grip."

With that admonishment ringing in her ears, Mia took her time in the shower, then moisturized and dried her hair completely. She was considering a manicure—anything to keep her away from him a little while longer—when she heard him talking to someone. She hesitated and realized he was on the phone. The tone of his voice was reserved, subdued, and she instinctively knew this conversation wasn't business-related.

A girlfriend? she thought, an irrational surge of jealousy making her muscles seize. It suddenly occurred to her that, though he had done a little subtle digging into her personal life, she had no idea what was actually going on in his. Mia straightened.

That would not do. Turnabout was fair play, after all.

He was sprawled on his bed, his back against the headboard, when she walked back into the room. His guarded gaze darted to hers, then drifted back to the television. Despite his seeming nonchalance, she could practically feel the tension hovering around him. "Yeah, it's good," he said. "I like it. Yeah, very different," he confirmed with a small laugh. He sighed, listening for a moment. "I'll try to come see you when I finish this assignment. I'm not sure, Mom. Next weekend, maybe. But—" he glanced at her, then away again "—it'll have to be neutral ground."

Neutral ground? Mia wondered, listening shamefully, unable to help herself. What did he mean by that?

"You know I can't come there. No, Mom, it hasn't been my home in a long, long time. Listen, I'll give you a call when I'm back in Atlanta, okay? We'll work something out then. Tell Gramps I'll call soon. I wasn't sure," he trailed off, then winced. "Yes, you're right. I should have known better." He paused, listened to something else his mother said that made him smile. "Yeah, Mom, I will. Love you, too." He disconnected and tossed the phone onto the bed, then rubbed the bridge of his nose.

A thousand questions burned on her tongue, but she determinedly withstood the fire. She busied herself by putting her toiletries away, then snagged her nail polish from her purse and began to touch up her toes.

"My mother," he said by way of explanation as the silence swelled between them.

Mia shot him a grin. "Believe it or not, I'd worked that one out for myself," she said, throwing his earlier words back at him.

Predictably, he chuckled and the strain in the air immediately lessened. His shoulders relaxed and he watched her, seemingly fascinated, as she dabbed paint onto her nails. "Sounds like she wants you to visit," Mia mused.

She'd met both of his parents when they'd been in college. His father had been friendly, but cold, and his mother had been a sweet woman who'd probably gone into her marriage with a backbone, but had lost it along the way. She'd never stood directly next to her husband, but had hung back a few inches. A telling gesture, one that indicated they weren't equal partners in their relationship.

"She does," he admitted. "I went directly to Atlanta when I left the military."

Mia merely hummed under her breath, hoping her silence would invite him to be more forthcoming. From what little she knew of his father, she didn't have any trouble understanding Tanner's "neutral ground" comment. How many times had Tanner told her he would be third-generation military? How often had she noticed his somewhat desperate attempts to earn his father's regard? She could only imagine the elder Crawford's response to his son ending his military service before retirement. What had prompted the decision wouldn't have mattered to his father, who would have, no doubt, seen the decision as one lacking in character. She peeked a glance at Tanner, who was still watching her paint her nails.

He would have known what his father's reaction would be, Mia thought, and yet he'd left the Rangers anyway. She gleaned more from that little insight than she had from the nightmares, and her heart ached for him in response.

"What's that?" he asked, a frown in his voice.

Mia capped the bottle, then bent forward a little more and blew on her wet nails. "What's what?"

"On the small of your back," he said, leaving his bed to get a better look. "A tattoo?" he said, a note of breathless shock in his voice. "You've got a tattoo?" His warm fingers nudged the fabric aside, eliciting a shiver from her.

Mia laughed and looked over her shoulder at him. "You seem surprised. What? You think you're the only one who can have one? You know the Poe Toaster was a no-show this year, right?" she added, wincing.

Tanner nodded grimly. "I'd heard. The first time since nineteen forty-nine. Sad, isn't it? Seeing the tradition come to an end."

"Maybe someone will pick it up," Mia offered. "It would be a shame if they didn't. Did you ever see him? I remember that you'd said you wanted to."

Tanner shook his head. "No. I'd planned to, though, now that I've got the time." He grimaced. "Guess I've left that too late, too."

"You never know," Mia said, trying to discern the undercurrent in his voice. There seemed to be a double meaning, but she couldn't figure out what precisely it was. "You should go next year," she suggested. "See what happens." She grinned. "They'll probably be several new Toasters vying to take on the tradition."

His gaze found hers and he smiled, but it was weak,

preoccupied. "True." He glanced down at the small of her back again. "'What's past is prologue,'" he quoted. "Shakespeare. *The Tempest,* right?"

She nodded, curiously short of breath. He was too close, too bare. Too damned sexy. All that warm male flesh was making her light-headed. She swallowed thickly. "Right."

Admiration clung to his smile. "Hidden depths," he murmured. "When did you get it?"

Ah, now came the tricky part. "Before I graduated," she said mildly. "It was an early present to me."

Something in his gaze shifted, grew more intuitive. That keen green gaze studied her until she had to forcibly resist the urge to squirm. "It's a great quote. Perfect for marking a new chapter in your life."

Yes, it was. It had marked *her* new chapter after *his* exit scene and, judging from the look on his face, he'd worked that out. She studied him levelly. "I thought so."

Actually, this was a good reminder, Mia thought. Tempted as she was to follow this attraction to its inevitable end, she was all too familiar with what would happen afterward. He would leave—again—and she would be devastated, undoubtedly needing another tattoo to denote the occasion. Something like "Fool me once, shame on you. Fool me twice, shame on me." And she'd have to put it down her arm or across her back to accommodate the size. She mentally grimaced. Unattractive.

Regret suddenly shadowed his eyes, making dread balloon in her belly. "Listen, Mia—"

Oh, no. Not another damned apology. The first one had been agonizing enough. She leaned away, lengthening the distance between them. "Oh, look!" she cried with feigned delight. "*While You Were Sleeping* is coming on. I love this movie." She settled more firmly against the headboard and turned an imploring gaze to him, full of enthusiasm she didn't feel. "Do you mind if we watch this?"

Tanner regarded her and, for one horrified moment, she was afraid he wasn't going to let it go, was going to insist on rehashing the past, particularly the bit where he'd broken her heart. Then his face relaxed and he smiled, hitching up a single corner of his mouth in that endearing grin of his. Her favorite, actually. "This is a chick flick, isn't it?"

"Yes."

He grimaced comically. "I thought so."

"You can choose the next one," she offered, then amended the gesture when a thought struck. She frowned. "So long as it's not porn."

Tanner chuckled and then tsked with regret. "Damn. And here I'd been looking forward to watching *The Penis Whisperer* with you."

Mia felt her eyes widen and she choked on a laugh. The Penis Whisperer? Lord, help her. "You'll live," she replied drolly.

Mia sighed. Whether she would or not until this was over remained to be seen.

9

WHAT'S PAST IS PROLOGUE, Tanner thought again as he watched Mia laugh at something on-screen. A tattoo she'd gotten right before they'd graduated…right around the time he'd broken up with her. A coincidence?

Possibly, but he didn't think so.

Despite the fact that she'd agreed with him when he'd told her things were moving too fast, he'd known that he'd hurt her, had even hated himself for it. But he hadn't understood the depth of the wound he'd inflicted until just a few moments ago.

Damn.

He was truly toxic, Tanner thought, self-disgust saturating every pore. And that was all the more reason he needed to keep his hands off her. The image of her bent over, hair hanging over one shoulder, painting her toes, her pink tongue sticking out as she concentrated on the process suddenly assailed him and he shifted because he'd gone so painfully hard.

Sexy didn't begin to cover it. She was unintentionally

provocative, effortlessly beautiful and so far removed from her own appeal it made her one of the most compellingly attractive women he'd ever been around. Factor in that keen mind, cutting wit and she became lethally fascinating.

It was piss-poor timing to be fascinated, Tanner thought.

Again.

And in light of that tattoo, he found himself more resolved than ever to be fair to her…and that meant keeping his hands to himself, no matter how damned hard—he glanced at his crotch and chuckled darkly—that became.

Determined to do just that, Tanner sent the backpack which housed Moe a disgruntled glance, then crossed his arms over his chest and closed his eyes. He drifted in and out of sleep, alternating waking to the sound of her soft laughter and dreaming strange dreams where they were back on campus, holding hands in front of Denny Chimes. Only in his dream, he was the one with the Shakespearean tattoo. It was inked down the inside of his right arm and, stranger still, she was wearing his Ranger beret. No, Tanner thought. No, she couldn't go. He wouldn't let her. He couldn't let her see the things he'd seen. The horror, the helplessness and the death.

A poor village, the tiny school, a series of blasts, then a scream.

His own, he realized as cool fingers slid over his brow. "Tanner, wake up," she said, her soothing voice rife with sympathy. "You're here. You're fine."

No, he wasn't. He was beginning to doubt he'd ever be fine again. The nightmares were merely punishment, a subconscious reprimand, for his part in what had happened outside Mosul. Logic told him that they couldn't have known that the insurgents would remote-detonate when his team arrived. But had they never arrived, it would have never happened. That was the part he couldn't get past, that no amount of logic could explain away. He'd followed orders, done what he'd been trained to do.

But nothing would ever make it right.

Continuing to shush him, Mia's small fingers moved over his brow, then traveled down the side of his cheek, slowly, almost reverently. He heard her release a deep, shaky sigh. Her touch held something he hadn't felt in too long to remember—since her, he imagined—and his chest inexplicably tightened.

Affection.

This girl had loved him, genuinely, truly, with every fiber of her being. Not because he'd been on the football team, not because he'd been a soldier. With no identifiers, with no qualifications, she'd just loved *him*…and he'd traded her heart for a beret.

He made a disgusted noise low in his throat and she mistook it for his continuing nightmare. She murmured another soothing noise, then leaned closer to him and kissed the corner of his eye.

And that was his undoing.

He looked up into her face, only inches from his own, then without saying a word, reached up and wound a long strand of hair around his finger. Her breathing caught and her liquid brown gaze searched his. The glow from the television cast bluish shadows on the walls and gilded the side of her face in light. She smelled like peaches, he realized, finally isolating the fruity scent. Ripe, sweet, smooth and slightly musky. It suited her.

With his gaze never leaving hers, he gave a gentle tug, bringing her closer, then bent forward and brushed his lips over hers. Her lush breast lay against his chest, her hand still on his face. He felt her shiver, soften, then he kissed her again and ate her low moan of capitulation.

Nothing had ever tasted more satisfying.

As though a switch had been flipped, she made a low, hungry growl in her throat, then crawled up and straddled him. Her hands framed his face and she kissed him deeply, while her sex rested perfectly over his. He nudged himself against her, smiled when he heard her gasp, and shaped his hands on the perfect globes of her rounded ass. Her waist was smaller than he'd realized, Tanner thought, as he mapped her body. He slid his fingers beneath the hem of her T-shirt and shuddered when he encountered bare skin.

She fed at his mouth, sucked at his tongue and pushed her hands into his hair. She shifted above him, drew back enough to let him bring her shirt over her head.

Bare breasts, dusky pearled nipples, creamy skin, delicate rib cage, womanly belly, long dark hair spilling over her pale shoulders to the small of her back.

Perfect. Utterly perfect.

He leaned forward and drew one rosy bud into his

mouth, shaped his hand around the other, testing the weight of it against his palm. She squirmed above him, settling more firmly against his dick and he lifted his hips in response, answering her silent plea.

He was breathing her in, absorbing her, tasting her and the rest of the world simply faded away. The room shrunk to the point that there was only him and her and the bed, and the night stretched out before them without end. She was a heavenly apparition after his own personal hell on earth and he just wanted her. Needed her. Had to have her.

She licked a trail down the side of his neck and slid her hands over his shoulders, leaving fire in their wake. Her palms were greedy, seemingly desperate for the feel of him. He suckled her harder and smiled when he heard her breathing catch. She worked herself against him, a firm steady slide along the length of him and it occurred to Tanner that this would feel a whole lot better to both of them if they were naked.

He reached blindly for the laptop case on the nightstand and withdrew the box of condoms—he made a mental note to thank Jamie Flanagan the next time he saw him—and laid several packages within easy reach.

In the process of tracing each of his ribs with her tongue, Mia looked over, spied the protection and made a humming noise. "I don't know whether to be annoyed or thankful," she murmured.

Tanner slid his hands beneath her pajama bottoms and pushed the distracting garment out of his way, filling his hands with her rear in the process and giving a squeeze.

Mia shuddered. "Thankful now," she said. "Annoyed later."

She rose long enough to kick the shorts off and Tanner took the opportunity to get out of his own boxers, as well.

Mia sat back on her haunches and her admiring gaze slid over the length of him. Her lids drooped with sleepy sensuality and he watched her pulse flutter wildly at the base of her throat. She licked her lips. "Where to start?"

He handed her a condom. "Can I make a suggestion?"

TANNER HAD ALWAYS BEEN a long, tall drink of water. At six and half feet, he towered over her and, while his size undoubtedly intimidated lesser men, she'd always found it unbelievably thrilling.

All that man, all that muscle…hers.

The idea that she could make him—all of him, every impossibly masculine part—want her had never been anything less than intoxicating. Looking at him now made her muscles melt, her spine go limp, her mouth water.

She ignored the condom in his outstretched hand—she knew exactly what he wanted to suggest, but they'd get to that soon enough—and took him in hand instead. She heard his breath hiss between his clenched teeth as he inhaled sharply.

She worked the slippery skin against her palm, marveling at the satiny feel over the hard shaft. Ridges and vein, the smooth rounded head… Tanner had been built on a monumental scale and this particular part of him was perfectly proportioned to the rest. Just feeling him in her hand made her belly clench, made her sex weep. A low throb built in her clit and tingled determinedly, a steady reminder of what she truly wanted.

All of him.

Inside of her.

It had been years since she'd had a proper orgasm, one that hadn't been self-manufactured, and the idea that the status quo was about to change left her feeling almost giddy with lust, light-headed with need. And the fact that it was Tanner, her original bell ringer, seemed strangely appropriate.

But even if it wasn't, she'd convince herself that it was because she just…wanted.

Him.

Though she'd wanted to play, to explore, to lick him from one end to the other, to feel every bit of muscle beneath her hands, feel his hair abrading her palms, to taste the tanned parts and the parts that weren't, Mia suddenly couldn't wait to put him between her legs, to feel the hardest part of him deep in the softest part of her. She'd explore later, but right now…

She tore into the condom, then swiftly rolled it into place.

…right now, she just wanted him inside of her.

Mia bent forward and settled herself against him,

coating him in her own wetness. A shiver rolled down her spine and she felt her neck prickle as exquisite sensation bolted through her. Tanner's gaze latched on to hers, his big hands anchored on her hips. She slid forward, then back, then tilted just so until she felt him nudge her outer channel.

She trembled, literally quaked from the inside out.

With a soft sigh of homecoming, she slowly impaled herself upon him. Tanner grimaced, as though the pleasure was almost unbearable and the sight of him—of his feral joy—tripped something deep inside of her. She lifted her hips, then settled onto him once more, feeling herself stretch to accommodate the size of him. He filled her so completely, so perfectly, she didn't know where she ended and he began and ultimately didn't care.

His big hands slid up over her hips, along her rib cage and then found her breasts. He bent forward and took the other nipple into his mouth, suckling as he thrust up and something about the combination released something wild inside of her. She felt the first flash of climax kindle in her womb and she tightened around him, clamping her feminine muscles.

Sensing her wordless cue, Tanner flattened the crown of her breast in his mouth, tickled the underside with his talented tongue, then took a deep pull and flipped her over onto her back. He left off her breast and ate her surprised gasp as he plunged into her.

Hot, hard male. Broad shoulders, sleek skin...

She bit into his shoulder and wrapped her legs around his waist, meeting him thrust for thrust as he plunged deeply and methodically into her body. His masculine hair abraded her nipples and he found her mouth, kissing her with the same rhythm, coupling every thrust below with a sweep of wonderful tongue. He was everywhere. On top of her, inside of her body, inside of her mouth, the smell of him in her nostrils, the feel of him beneath her hands. She was drugged, already an addict, hooked on him.

He pounded harder, then faster and faster still and she arched against him, absorbing every powerful plunge into her body. He'd already lit a fire within her and with every stroke, like a puff of air against a new flame, he fanned the blaze, swiftly creating an inferno that she knew was going to char her from the inside out.

He kissed her again, pushed harder, then reached down and lifted her hips, putting her an angle that instantly made everything...more.

More wonderful, more intense, more amazing.

That flash of climax she'd felt earlier suddenly peaked and she came hard. Mia inhaled deeply, felt every muscle in her body go rigid. Her mouth opened in a soundless scream of pleasure, then a moan ripped from her throat, a noise she would have never imagined she was capable of.

She heard Tanner chuckle, a pleased, masculine sound, then he pumped more frantically into her, milking her release for every bit of sensation. She clamped around him repeatedly, reached around and grabbed his ass, pushing him deeper and suddenly he tensed, angled higher and planted himself as far into her as he possibly could. A bellow of pure satisfaction rumbled from his chest and she felt her own feminine smile of satisfaction slide over her lips.

When the last tremor shook his body, he rolled off her, taking her with him. Then he discarded the condom and settled her firmly into the crook of his arm.

She trailed her fingers over his chest, more satisfied than she could ever recall being. And that included the last time they'd done this. For reasons she couldn't explain, it was better this time around. Possibly because now she knew how rare good sex truly was.

"That feels nice," he murmured.

She smiled. "I hope the rest of it wasn't a waste of time then."

He chuckled softly and pressed a kiss against her head. "Not totally."

She pinched him playfully. "Idiot."

He laughed and gave her a squeeze, then relaxed more fully against her. "We've wasted a lot of time, but the last little bit we got *completely* right."

She nuzzled his neck with her nose and silently agreed, satisfaction saturating every pore. Rather than spoil the moment with all the reasons she shouldn't have allowed this to happen, Mia simply cuddled closer to him and let the sound of his heartbeat lull her to sleep. Regret and heartbreak were certainly on the horizon, but until it actually arrived, she was going to borrow a page from Scarlett O'Hara's book and think about it tomorrow.

Tanner kissed her head again. "Mia?"

"Hmm."

"Thanks."

She knew he wasn't talking about the sex. "You're welcome."

10

TANNER AWOKE THE NEXT morning with a handful of breast, a soft bottom against his loins and the overwhelming impression that something good had happened to him last night.

Oh, yeah.

Mia.

She stirred against him, made a sleepy noise that resonated curiously in his own chest. The room smelled like peaches and sex and there was a contentedness in his bones that he hadn't felt in a long, long time.

She rolled her head to face him, and smiled groggily. "Morning," she murmured. If she had any regrets, then she hid them well. He released a breath he hadn't realized he'd been holding. "Did we miss our wake-up call?" she asked.

He laughed and absently thumbed her nipple. "Do we care?"

She pressed her rump against him. "Hmm. I guess not."

That was all the invitation he needed, Tanner thought.

He snagged a condom, sheathed himself first in it, and then with a low guttural groan, in *her.*

She gasped and arched back, lifting her leg to give him better access. She grabbed his thigh and gave a squeeze as he slowly pushed in and out of her, savoring her this time. She was tight and wet and ready. Sexy as hell. "I p-prefer this s-sort of wake-up call," she said brokenly.

He reached around her, found the little kernel nestled at the top of her sex and stroked. "Me, too," he murmured.

She gasped, wiggled against him, already so close to coming for him. She was so responsive, so uninhibited. She knew what made her feel good and didn't care if it was undignified or unseemly. She simply *enjoyed.* He bent forward and nibbled on her ear, upped the pressure against her clit and thrust harder.

Predictably, she shattered around him, convulsing so hard that her release triggered his own. The orgasm caught him off guard, blasted out of his loins so hard that his vision actually blackened around the edges. His legs went weak and he growled low in her ear.

"You know what I wish?" she murmured. "I wish it wasn't anatomically impossible for you to be between my legs and in my mouth at the same time."

His jaw went slack with that bald statement and, in the time it took him to gather his wits, she'd disentangled herself from him and gone into the bathroom. He heard the shower come on.

*Warm, wet and naked womanly skin. Painted toes,
Shakespeare stamped on the small of her back...*

Why was he still in bed?

He bolted up and headed for the bathroom. The scent
of peaches and minty toothpaste assailed his senses and
he caught a glimpse of a womanly silhouette outlined
behind the curtain. He went hard again.

She chuckled, a wicked sound that curled around his
senses. "I wondered how long it would take you to join
me."

Tanner quickly brushed his teeth, then nudged the
curtain aside and climbed into the shower with her. She
was rosy already, her creamy skin heated and flushed.
From the shower? he wondered, or their previous bed
play? Ultimately, it didn't matter. She was gorgeous,
a siren, and he needed her more now than he had last
night.

Mia looped her arms around his neck, leaned up and
kissed him, slowly, deeply. She pushed her hands into
his hair, then trailed them over his neck and shoulders,
growling low with approval as her hands feasted on him.
She made him feel powerful and beastly, more caveman
than gentleman. Her mouth left off his, then trailed its
way over his chest, her facile tongue flicking a nipple.

He shuddered, unaware of the erogenous zone.

She slid her fingers over his arms, made her way
around his back and kissed his shoulders. Her hot mouth
made a line down his spine, then she gently turned him
around and took him into her mouth. She looked up

at him then, those melting chocolate eyes beneath wet lashes, her ripe pink mouth closing around his dick…

If he'd ever seen anything sexier in his life, he couldn't recall it.

Nothing was hotter than having a woman who actually wanted to taste you. And Mia did. Her eyes fluttered shut as she took the whole of him into her mouth, sliding her tongue along the underside of his dick. She took a long draw and massaged his balls, then licked and sucked her way from one end of him to the other, over and over again, like he was the last ice-cream cone of the season.

Tanner braced one hand against the side of the shower and grabbed the rail with the other. Every muscle in his body was alternately seizing up and going limp as she quite literally ate him. Pink lips, pinker tongue wrapped around him. She suckled the root of him, then took a ball into her mouth and rolled it over her tongue as though savoring the best dessert she'd ever had. It was that sheer joy that ultimately did it for him and he drew back.

She caught him, guided him back into her mouth, then did something phenomenal with the skin right behind his balls.

He came so hard he pulled the shower curtain off the rod. The only thing that prevented him from collapsing was the idea that she'd stop doing whatever it was that she was doing.

When the last contraction shook from his body, she slowly stood and licked her slightly swollen lips.

Wearing a cat in the cream pot smile, she gestured to the shower curtain and tsked. "You're going to have to pay for that."

Still trying to catch his breath, Tanner merely smiled down at her. "Gladly."

He quickly reattached the curtain as best he could, then bent and nuzzled the side of her neck. Her eyes closed, she smiled. "That feels nice."

"Brace yourself, baby, because what I'm about to do is going to feel even better." He kicked her feet apart, then dropped to his knees and attached his mouth to her sex. She was velvety soft against his tongue and her womanly taste exploded over his palette.

She groaned and her knees trembled, threatening to buckle.

He smiled against her.

He licked and laved, paying special attention to little nub of sensation at the top, then inserted a finger deep within her channel and began to stroke.

She squirmed against him, reaching up and grabbing hold of the rod. But she was so short, he knew it was a stretch for her. "Put your leg up here," he said, indicating the side of the tub.

Amazingly, without argument, she did. "And you call me Bossy," she said, her voice raw with longing.

He tented his tongue over her clit and methodically stroked, coupling the rhythm of his finger with that of his mouth. He felt her contract around him and knew she was close.

"Inside me," she whispered brokenly. "I need you inside me. You don't know— It's been so long— I—"

Tanner stood, filled his hands with her ripe breasts and pushed into her from behind.

Hot, silky skin enclosed him and he locked down every muscle to keep from coming right then. Too late he realized his mistake and he swore hotly. "Mia, I didn't bring a condom. I—"

"You'd better have a clean bill of health, otherwise I'm going to unman you." She clenched around him, betraying the threat with her own body's response.

"I do."

"So do I and I'm protected."

Profound relief swept through him and he rested his head between her shoulders, then pushed up into her again. Her body tightened around his, signaling a need that was deep-seated and old as time itself.

It was the first time in years that he'd had unprotected sex—in fact, the last time had been with her in the library—and the sensation was almost more than he could bear. Sex in any case was good, but going bare into a woman, feeling skin on intimate skin...

It was beyond amazing. Unequalled.

And Mia felt so damned good. He pushed into her, pounded harder and harder, the water at his back, her at his front, her beautiful round rear end against him as he thrust repeatedly into her welcoming heat.

She grunted and groaned, made all sorts of nonsensical little sounds that told him without words how much she was enjoying this, how much she loved the feel of having him inside of her.

It turned him on more than anything else, this knowing that he was lighting her up, that she needed him as much as he needed her, that this unholy attraction wasn't now nor ever had been one-sided.

She suddenly clamped around him, her feminine muscles seizing, and she screamed his name.

His name.

He came again, even harder than before.

Whether he'd marked her or she'd marked him, Tanner didn't know. All he knew was that this was right.

She was right.

And that was all that ultimately mattered.

MIA WASN'T QUITE SURE when she'd turned into such a wanton, but she had to admit she rather liked it. It was fun to say exactly what she thought, to do exactly what she'd been thinking about for years. Tanner was like her own personal sex toy and, though she knew a reckoning would come when they arrived in Dallas and parted ways, she'd decided that she was going to ride out the rest of this trip exactly as she wanted to.

Selfish? Stupid? Foolhardy?

Yes, to all of the above, but dammit, she was due. Or at least that was what she was going to tell herself. It sounded so much better than "desperate" and "deprived."

She just wanted him. And since he wanted her, too, she honestly wasn't going to look too closely for the harm. They had, at best, another couple of days. And forewarned was forearmed, right? There was no expectation on her part this time because she knew he had no intention of sticking around.

Strange how their lives kept intersecting at the wrong time. In college he'd had his gaze attached firmly to his career and, though she'd registered in his peripheral vision, she'd never been able to shift the focus enough to include her.

This time around, he was in the process of putting his life back together, starting over in a new career, hounded by nightmares and an estranged relationship with his father. Now wasn't their time, either, Mia knew, but damn how she wished it could be.

The horrible truth was that Tanner Crawford had always owned a little part of her heart and she'd never gotten it back. The memory of him, of what he'd meant to her, had always hovered on the fringes, reminding her of what could have been. What truly loving someone was all about. Her gaze slid to him, where he sat next to her in the SUV.

Other guys had come and gone, but only *this one* had touched her soul. Only *this one* had laid her bare, made her vulnerable.

As though somehow managing to read her thoughts, Tanner squeezed her hand. "Do you have any idea how frustrating this is?"

She blinked. "How frustrating what is?"

"You're being too quiet. I get nervous when you get quiet. It means you're thinking."

He sounded so ominous she had to laugh. "And my thinking scares you?"

His gaze slid back to the road. A big red barn with a John Deere logo painted on the roof loomed in the distance and cows dotted the landscape behind barbed-wire fences. "Depends on what you're thinking about."

Ah. So that was what was driving him nuts. He wanted to be in her head. Too damned bad, Mia thought. Being in her heart was going to have to do. She was sharing her body with him, her time, everything else that she had.

Her thoughts, though, were going to have to be her own.

"I'm thinking that I'm hungry, if you must know," she improvised. She shoved her knitting back into her bag and flexed her fingers.

"You're not sorry, then? No regrets?"

Now this was a new side, a rather endearing one, actually. He was nervous. "Tanner, if I'd had any regrets, you would have woken up alone this morning, not with my ass squished up against your privates," she remarked drolly. "Furthermore, the shower should have erased any lingering doubts as to whether or not I had any regrets." She heaved a long-suffering sigh. "Much as it pains me to admit it, I find you sexually irresistible."

He looked pleased for about five seconds, then his smile slowly capsized. "Wait a minute. Are you telling me that you only want me for my body?" He grunted and drummed his thumb against the wheel. "I had no idea you'd grown so shallow."

She shrugged, playing along. "You've been gone a long time. There's a lot you don't know."

He sent her a glance. "That sounds extremely cryptic."

She winced dramatically. "Damn, I was aiming for mysterious."

She waited, knowing her silence would get to him.

"Okay," he said with a sigh. "I'll bite. What do I not know?"

"Are you sure this is a conversation you want to have?" she asked him, sending him a sidelong glance. "You've been a lot less forthcoming about what you've been doing the past ten years than I have, you know."

"Fair warning, eh?" he said, insightful as usual. "You're going to want tit for tat?"

Mia took a sip of her drink and popped a few peanuts into her mouth. "I don't know that fair warning is exactly right, but I'd advise you not to ask me any questions you wouldn't want asked in return. I haven't pried, but if you're going to, then so am I."

He paused, seeming to consider her for a moment. "I've appreciated that more than you know, Mia. Any other woman would have cross-examined me like a hostile witness by now and yet...you haven't."

Touched, she swallowed. "Not because I haven't been curious, I can assure you," she told him. "But I figure there are very few things that we genuinely get to own in our lives and pain, at the very least, should be one of them." She meant it. Grief was personal, much more so than sex or love or anything else, in her opinion.

Something in his gaze shifted, softened. "You know, that's one of the things I always loved about you. You're intuitive. You get me." A little sigh slipped past his lips. "You always did."

Something like regret colored his tone, giving her the first glimpse into how he'd truly felt about her. Her heart lightened, making her feel less foolish. Maybe it hadn't been as easy for him to leave her as she'd thought, Mia decided.

"Okay," he said. "Your warning is dully noted. Now… have you ever married?"

She chuckled, relieved. "That's the burning question? That's what's been bugging you?"

"Yes. I seem to remember that it used to be pretty important to you."

She couldn't tell him the truth, that no one else had ever measured up. That it had taken years for her to even consider another long-term relationship, much less marriage. And it *had* been important to her. She'd wanted the whole thing, the burning romance, the passion, someone to trust, to love. She'd wanted a family. It had been hard for Mia to watch her mother do it all alone. And, though her mother had never complained, it had to have been even harder for her. Funny the things you appreciate more as an adult than you ever did as a teenager. Her father, the only man she'd ever really had in her life had been a loser. Was it so terrible to want a good one? An honorable one? Was she wrong to want a real family?

But to answer his question… "No, I haven't."

"Why not?"

"Priorities shift," she murmured evasively. "I fell in love with history, with my job. It hasn't left much room for anything else." *You ruined me for anyone else. I stopped waiting for lightning to strike twice.*

"What about superlover Harlan?" he asked, his lip curling with distaste. "You never wanted the white picket fence and minivan with him?"

Mia smothered a snicker. That jab about Harlan and his so-called sexual prowess had definitely hit the mark. Superlover Harlan? She cleared her throat to cover a laugh. "No," she said. "I told you that we could never quite make the happily-ever-after idea gel."

He stared straight ahead. "So you don't want it anymore? Is that what you're saying?"

She couldn't imagine why he was so interested. If memory served, that had never been his dream, even when it had been hers. He'd wanted to be a Ranger, to follow in his grandfather and father's footsteps. Even football hadn't mattered as much as chasing the military dream, one that, from the looks of things, had recently quite literally turned into a nightmare.

"It's grown a bit dusty," she admitted truthfully. "But I suppose if the right person ever came along, I'd be willing to pull it down off the shelf and polish it up a bit." In all honesty, the only "right person" had ever been him and considering how unlikely his sticking around was, she didn't see the point in even allowing herself to entertain the idea. It was too…difficult. It made her want to look at what-might-have-been and examine the if-only's.

Water under a bridge that had burned.

"What about you?" she asked, turning the question around on him. She stared at the wildflowers growing alongside the road. Black-eyed Susan's and Queen Anne's lace, the occasional poppy. "Did you ever marry?"

He chuckled and shook his head. "Nah, never even came close. The job wasn't conducive to dating, much less building any kind of a permanent relationship."

"Was it worth it?" she asked, hoping he didn't detest the hint of bitterness that leaked into her voice.

Tanner turned to look at her, his gaze inscrutable and a weary smile formed on his mouth. "Ultimately... no."

And with that shockingly glib comment, he pulled off the highway into the parking lot of a series of buildings—an old gas station, a seed and feed store, a small antiques shop and a little barbecue joint that promised a sauce "hot enough to melt the wax outta your ears."

Which was good, considering hers were still ringing from his honesty, a truth she'd never expected.

Tanner Crawford had many regrets and, from the sounds of things, *she* was one of them.

Breaking news: Hell had frozen over.

Funny then that her heart had thawed.

11

"Do you mind if we go into the antiques shop before we eat?" she asked as she climbed out of the car.

The bag holding Moe securely over his arm, Tanner looked down at her, watching her stretch. It was nice. "I thought you said you were starving."

"I said I was hungry, but—" she nodded toward the old building "—that looks promising."

He shot a skeptical glance in the direction she indicated. A bottomless chair and an old wringer washer sat outside, along with a clump of ancient school desks and various gardening tools. A rusty sign over the door said Bubba's Antique Mall, Pawnshop and Taxidermy.

Promising was not the description he would have used to describe it, but he'd indulge her. "Come on," he said, slinging an arm over her shoulder. "To the junk store we go."

Despite not traveling via the interstate, they were still making excellent progress. He suspected the GPS had bought them the time they'd needed to go off radar.

Ackerman and Ramirez knew their ultimate destination, of course, but he'd already been thinking about extra precautions he would take going into Dallas.

She tsked under her breath, but smiled all the same and that grin did something funny to his chest. Made it feel lighter and fuller than it had in years. "One man's trash is another man's treasure," she admonished. "Haven't you ever heard that before?"

He grunted as he opened the door, the scent of old stuff and pipe tobacco wafting to him on a hot breeze. "One man's trash is another fool's garbage," Tanner told her, his gaze immediately drawn to the stuffed armadillo on the long counter. Ghastly.

"Shut up," she said, laughing softly. "This is my kind of store. More than half the stuff in my house has come from places like this. You never know what you're going to find."

"Don't tell me you have a stuffed armadillo in your house."

She shushed him, immediately drawn to an assortment of old dishes. "Of course, not. Just let me look for a few minutes," she said. "I'll hurry."

Tanner picked up a pair of salt and pepper shakers in the shape of pigs and shook his head. "Take your time," he told her.

She nodded, too distracted with a dark blue iced-tea pitcher to heed him. His cell phone suddenly vibrated at his waist, snagging his attention. "Crawford," he answered.

"It's Payne. I've sent the information you requested regarding Mia's father to you via e-mail."

"Good," Tanner said. "I appreciate it. Anything interesting turn up? Any connection to Ramirez?"

"Not directly, no," Payne told him. "But his last address was in New Orleans—"

"Ramirez's home turf," Tanner interjected.

"—and he'd clocked six months in a parish jail for narcotics possession."

"Dealing, you think?"

"Possibly," Payne said. "He's got a record a mile long. Mostly petty theft, but there's a couple of drug charges, assault and battery and cruelty to animals. Dog fighting. He's a nasty bit of work and he's been in Mia's area. He picked up a speeding ticket outside Alexandria two weeks ago. Has she mentioned seeing him?"

"No, not in D.C., anyway. She thought she saw him yesterday, though, which is why I asked for the background check. Did you happen to get a list of visitors from the jail?"

"It's in the file. He's quite the ladies' man. He had several women coming to see him, bringing him books and cigarettes. None of the names rung a bell, but you might have better luck. I managed to pull driver's license photos on most of them."

"Thanks, Payne."

"Let me know if you need anything else."

Tanner told him he would, then disconnected before his employer could ask him any other questions. Though Payne hadn't said a word, Tanner could hear the distant curiosity in his voice. Or maybe that was just his own guilty conscience. At any rate, he looked forward to accessing that file. They'd need to stop at a coffee shop with Internet access soon so that he could take a look. He hated that Mia's father had become a suspect of sorts, but at this point, no one was above suspicion.

He wandered over to where Mia stood, poring over a jewelry case, a small photo in her hand.

"What are you doing?" he asked.

"Just looking," she murmured.

"For something specific?"

"You'll think I'm crazy."

"I know you're crazy," he told her. "It's part of your charm. What are you looking for?"

Mia sighed and handed him the photo. It had been enlarged to show a woman's hand, a ring on her fourth finger. "This," she said. "I always look, keep hoping I'll get lucky."

Tanner inspected the ring. It was quite different. A big opal surrounded by diamonds and rubies. "This was your mother's?"

"Yes," she said, releasing a sigh as she straightened away. "It had belonged to her grandmother. My dad pawned it…and I've never stopped looking. Crazy, huh? I know the odds of me ever finding that ring are practically nonexistent, but I can't *not* look. I *always* look."

Another reason to pummel her father, Tanner thought. He swallowed back his anger, hoping to keep his voice passably even. "That's not crazy, Mia. That's admirable."

Her gaze softened and she smiled up at him. "Thank you," she said. "Do you know, I think that's one of the nicest things anyone has ever said to me?"

He slid a finger down her cheek, reveling in the softness. "Then people need to try harder. Did you find anything you want?"

Something shifted behind her gaze—anguish, maybe?—but vanished before he could properly identify it.

"Nah," she said. "Let's go get something to eat."

Ten minutes later, Tanner chased a bite of the wickedly hot barbecue with a drink of iced tea and tried to pretend like his mouth wasn't on fire.

Mia wasn't buying it. "Fool," she said, sending him a glare. "I told you not to get the flaming hot sauce. I don't know what you thought you had to prove." She said it with indulgent affection, the kind brought about by familiarity and intimacy. Something moved around in his chest when he looked at her, something beautiful and terrifying.

"Who said I was trying to prove anything?" Tanner wheezed, wondering if his insides were getting charred as much as his mouth. He seriously couldn't feel his lips anymore. Bad sign. "I happen to like spicy food."

She rolled her eyes. "Can you even taste it?"

He tried to smile, but wasn't sure he succeeded. "I tasted the first bite."

She just shook her head. "Idiot."

"Fool, idiot," he repeated, placing a hand over his heart. "I love these little pet names you have for me.

They make me feel special. Cherished and respected, even."

Her lips twitched. "Beats the hell out of Bossy," she said. "I am not bossy. I just like telling people what to do."

He laughed. "I hate to break it to you, sweetheart, but the two kind of go hand in hand." He tossed her one of the disposable phones. "You should probably check in with Sophie. See how things are in Dallas."

She swallowed, poked her fork into her baked beans but didn't readily take a bite. "Will we get there tonight?"

"We can," he said haltingly. "But we'd be pushing it. I thought we'd stop in Texarkana, then finish the drive in the morning. We'd get in around noon. Is that okay with you?"

Tanner waited for her answer and tried to pretend like it didn't matter. Truth be told, he'd originally planned to push on through, to finish the drive tonight. He could have deposited her and Moe in Dallas, then caught a red-eye back to Atlanta. He would have successfully completed his first mission for Ranger Security.

But, selfishly, he wanted one more night with her. He wanted to spend the evening tasting every inch of her body, listening to those sweet, sexy sounds she made when he pushed into her, or suckled her breasts. He wanted to take her hard and fast against the wall, then stretch her out on the bed and make love to her until he couldn't move or breathe or think or, God help him, dream. He wanted one perfect, unspoiled night with her.

She was his light in the darkness. She made him feel lighter, better, less damaged and more in control. She was his hope, Tanner realized, and he wasn't ready to give her up.

Not yet.

He knew it wasn't fair to drag her into his life right now, to taint her with his gloom, but he was too selfish not to. He would have to let her go, of course, because it was the right thing to do. Their time had passed. He'd blown it then and couldn't ask for a do over now, not when he was emotionally condemned, practically disinherited from his family. He was a wreck, the pieces still scattered around his feet.

She could put him to rights, Tanner knew, but it wouldn't be fair to ask her. After the way he'd treated her, after he'd broken her heart and left her alone to put it back together, how could he? What right did he have? Admittedly, he knew he was a selfish bastard, but even selfish bastards could be noble. When the time came, he would dredge his soul for that character trait and do what must be done.

He wouldn't hurt her again. He'd let her blame it all on Moe, and he'd walk away before her life became as unrecognizable as his own.

Right girl, wrong time.

Again.

"Noon should be fine," she said. "And you'll return immediately to Atlanta, right?"

He nodded. "Yes. I'm going to check in there, do some unpacking. All of my stuff is currently stacked in the spare bedroom. The apartment's nice—beats the hell out of the barracks, that's for damned sure," he said, rubbing a hand over the back of his neck. "But it won't feel like home until I've put some of my Daniel Moores in place." The prints by the legendary painter were of some of his favorites, *Crimson Legacy and The Tradition Continues,* in particular. Famous for capturing great moments in sports history, Moore was highly talented and even more collectible.

Mia looked up and smiled. "Roll Tide roll. I've been to a few games," she said. "But I haven't been back as much as I'd like. I made homecoming last year."

"I haven't been back at all." He arched a brow. "Sad, isn't it?"

"It's not too far a drive from Atlanta to Tuscaloosa," she pointed out.

"It's not too far from Savannah to Atlanta, either," he said. "Maybe you could come over and go to a game with me."

His cell rang phone before she could answer and he mentally swore. He checked the caller ID and looked up at Mia. "This is my sister," he said, frowning. "I'd better take it."

She nodded. "Of course."

Because he didn't want to leave her or Moe alone, Tanner simply sat there and made the decision to try and be as vague as possible while talking to Roxanne.

"Hey, Roxy."

"Our father is a miserable bastard," she said, greeting him.

Tanner chuckled softly, watched a little gathering of birds peck at the crumbs beneath the picnic table. "You'll get no argument from me there."

"Mom's left him."

Shock detonated through him. "What?"

"She packed her bags and moved in with Aunt Margaret. I told her that she was welcome to come here, but she said she didn't want to be in the way. She's already bought a lot in Margaret's retirement community and picked out a house plan. They break ground next week."

Tanner didn't know what to say. "I—"

"Shocked, aren't you? She's worried about what you'll think and she doesn't want you to feel responsible. But evidently Dad's treatment of you for leaving the service was the final nail in the moldy coffin. She said she'd lost all respect for him and that you couldn't love someone you couldn't respect. She told me to tell you not to worry anymore about neutral ground. She'll soon have her own ground for you to visit on and that our father can kiss her ass."

He felt his eyes bug. He'd never heard his mother say anything harsher than "dang." "Mom cussed?" he breathed.

Roxy laughed delightedly. He could hear his nephew, Eli, babbling in the background, some sort of children's show entertaining him. "She did. She's been cussing a lot, actually." She paused. "I don't know about you, but I'm damned proud of her."

"I am, too, Roxy. Shocked, but pleased for her if it's what she wants."

"She said it's been a long time coming."

He could certainly believe that. His father had never treated her with the respect she deserved. Hell, the man never treated *anyone* who had the misfortune of orbiting through his life with the respect they deserved.

"Wow," he said, for lack of anything better.

"I know. So when can we expect you? Any chance you can make it this weekend? Gramps is hurt, you know. He said you ought to know better than to assume that he's going to be anything other than proud of you."

Tanner swallowed, momentarily unable to speak. "Not this weekend," he said, his gaze sliding over to Mia who was pretending not to listen and failing miserably. The sun glinted off her mink locks, painting copper highlights on her crown. "But soon, okay. Tell Mom and Gramps it won't be long. And give Eli a hug for me."

"He loves the football you sent him," Roxy said. "But you know you're going to have to teach him how to play with it. I love Mark dearly, but he doesn't have an athletic bone in his body."

Tanner chuckled. "Give the man a little bit of credit. He can throw a football."

"He can't throw one like you can," she said fondly. "Eli misses you."

Tanner laughed, even as he could feel himself succumbing to the guilt trip. "He's eighteen months old and doesn't even know me."

"My point exactly. Come home, Tanner. We miss you." *Guilt Central.*

Tanner smiled and passed a hand over his face. "I will, sis. Soon, I promise."

"Good. Now call Mom and let her know that you're proud of her. She needs to hear it from you, not from me. Gramps, too."

"I will."

"Will you do it now, so I won't have to call you and nag?" she needled shamelessly.

He laughed. "Yes."

"Love you, big brother."

"Love you, too, sis."

He ended the call and sat there for a moment, trying to absorb a world where his parents were separated.

"Something wrong?" Mia asked.

"No," he said. "My mother has left my father."

She blinked. "And that's not wrong?"

His lips formed a humorless smile. "You met my father. What do you think?"

She chewed the inside of her cheek and nodded. "Good for your mom. Anything particular prompt her decision?"

Tanner winced and looked away. "You're getting less shy with your questions."

"Sorry," she said. "I meant to pry, but was hoping you'd answer without noticing."

Tanner felt a smile drift over his lips. "I never answer anything without noticing."

She grimaced adorably. "So I noticed."

Tanner hesitated, wondered how much he could say without breaking out into a cold sweat. He cleared his throat. "Let's just say that my dad was not happy with my decision to leave the military."

She rolled her eyes and her lips formed a small smile. "Believe it or not, having met your father, I'd actually worked that one out for myself."

Of course she had, Tanner thought. Mia didn't miss a trick. "Yes, well, he's been quite vocal with his displeasure and has essentially disowned me for my 'cowardice and weakness.' In his words, I've disgraced him."

Her gaze hardened and he watched her jaw move back and forth, as though she were grinding her teeth. "So am I correct in guessing that your mother pulled the sanctimonious stick out of his ass and beat him with it?"

Tanner chuckled, startled at her description. "In a manner of speaking, yes. She's left him. In fact, she's already bought a lot and is building a house in my aunt Margaret's retirement community." She would probably learn to play bridge and join the Garden Club. And she would bloom, Tanner knew.

"Good for her," Mia said, nodding once. Her gaze found his and she leaned forward. "Look, Tanner, I don't know what happened that made you want to leave the military, but I know *you*," she said, taking his hand. "And you have more integrity in your little finger than your father does in his whole body. There is nothing—*nothing*—cowardly about you. You are not weak and you're not a disgrace. I don't have to know the particulars to know that." She squeezed his hand. "You're a good man, Tanner. You always have been."

Tanner swallowed hard. "How can you, of all people, say that? I treated you abominably."

She merely stared at him, seeming to be measuring her response, weighing the edited version against the unabridged. "You broke my heart," she said levelly, clearly opting for the latter. "I won't deny it. I was head over heels in love with you and would have followed you to the ends of the earth and back again." She paused. "But you stayed true to your path, true to your own vision of how you wanted your life to be. How could I fault you for that?" She smiled sadly. "I was the one who was willing to compromise. How could I crucify you for not willing to be? You stayed *you*. *I* was the one who changed and that was nobody's fault but my own."

A weak smile slid over his lips. "I never deserved you."

She grinned. "I know." She jerked her head toward his phone. "Don't you need to call your mother?"

He shook his head. "Bossy," he muttered.

"You secretly like it."

"Then it's a secret to me."

She tossed a potato chip at him, hitting him in the chin. "Asshole."

He sighed again. "Another charming endearment."

She leaned forward and pressed a lingering kiss against his lips. "It's good seeing you again," she said. "Believe it or not, I've missed you."

·He did believe it, which was going to make it harder than ever to leave.

In fact, it was going to be damned near impossible.

PUTTING THE TRACKING DEVICE on a semi bound for Omaha had been a crafty thing for Mia's travel companion to do, and the man applauded the ingenuity, no matter how much of an inconvenience it had caused him. He'd wasted a lot of time and a lot of gas, but ultimately he would prevail. He knew the name of the man Mia travelled with, knew that he'd just left the military.

More importantly, he knew *why* he'd left the military.

Weaknesses, when dealing with adversaries, was key and he'd learned Tanner Crawford's.

The only possible reason Mia could be traveling with a security agent was if she—or they—were carrying something he needed to protect. And considering the backpack never left the security agent's body, the man grimly suspected what was in it. Anticipation spiked. He slid a finger over the barrel of his gun and laughed low.

And the minute they arrived in Dallas, it would be his…no matter who tried to get in his way.

DAMN HIS FATHER, Mia thought. Miserable, awful old bastard. She'd suspected as much—that he'd not responded kindly to Tanner's leaving the military—but hearing Tanner repeat his father's words in that toneless voice had been gut-wrenchingly horrible.

Though she had a general idea of what had happened to make Tanner want to leave the service—and only then, due to those horrible nightmares—she knew him well enough to know that it had to have been beyond terrible to make him abandon the career he'd worked so hard for. It had to have been unendurable, otherwise he would have done just that.

Endured.

Though this trip going off without a hitch was important to her job, Mia knew that it was ultimately more important for Tanner. He was trying to rebuild a life, one that had been blown apart by war and exacerbated by a father who didn't appreciate him.

She was beginning to think fathers, on the whole, were overrated.

Though she could tell that he hadn't wanted to mention it to her, Tanner had shown her the information Ranger Security had dug up on her father.

It was depressing as hell.

He was even worse than she remembered, and his being in D.C. as early as a couple of weeks ago gave her pause. After a few moments of agonizing angst, Mia had finally drummed up the courage to call Harlan and ask him about what her father had specifically said when he'd called. He'd claimed to have gotten the number from someone at the Center, which Mia knew to be completely untrue. There was no way in hell anyone at the Center would have given out her phone number, even if it had been a person claiming to be her father.

Either he'd become more crafty through his time spent in jail, or he had better connections.

Or both.

Harlan said he'd seemed more interested in knowing what Mia was doing than actually seeing her. Her former boyfriend hadn't told her because he hadn't wanted to hurt her feelings. He'd put her father off, because that's what she'd asked him to do. When asked if Charlie had called in the past few days, Harlan said he didn't think so. If he had, then Harlan hadn't talked to him.

Much as she wanted to believe otherwise, she was beginning to suspect her father had something to do with the attempted thefts. According to Tanner, Charlie had been in New Orleans jail until three months ago. New Orleans was Ramirez's stomping ground. Furthermore, her father had always been a charming fellow—she'd looked at the pictures of women who'd visited him in jail, but hadn't recognized any of them—and he'd always been much more able to get information out of people than Freddie Ackerman, she would imagine.

But that still didn't explain why Freddie had been the one to follow them.

Her head aching from all the possibilities, Mia tossed her purse onto the bed then toed her shoes off and flexed her feet. They were swollen from spending so much time in the car. Though she'd wanted to have another night with Tanner, she had to admit she would have wanted to stop for the night anyway, rather than push on. She was tired and wearied of being in the car.

Per Tanner's instruction, she'd checked in with

Sophie, who had assured her that everything there was running smoothly. "No hiccups," she said, to which Mia had been eternally thankful. Since getting the new rental car and putting all of Tanner's safety measures in place, they'd continued on without incident. They would arrive in Dallas tomorrow, Moe in hand, and she could give him over and breathe a deep sigh of relief that they'd all made the journey safely.

She refused to consider what would happen afterward. It was too damned depressing.

But sadly, inevitable.

"Something wrong?" Tanner asked, glancing up to see her frown.

Mia glanced around the room, noting the same pictures, the same drapes, the same linens as the last motel and shot Tanner a smile. "Do you have some form of OCD or are you just really brand loyal?"

He smiled. "What are you talking about?"

"Same motel chain, same location on the floor and in some cases, the same room number. Are you building points for a vacation? Trying to get some perks? What?"

Tanner chuckled and shook his head. "It's a safety measure." he said. "Bottom floor, nearest the exit. This hotel offered the best layout for monitoring or making a quick escape if need be." His eyes twinkled. "I would have expected you to work that one out on your own. You're usually much quicker."

She couldn't argue with that. She'd completely missed the significance.

"You're off your game, Bossy. Something wrong?" he asked.

"Just tired," she said, which wasn't strictly a lie. As for her game, she wasn't just off it—she'd lost it completely.

Tanner sauntered over, a wicked grin on his lips, and plopped down onto the bed bedside her. "I hope you catch your second wind," he told her. He fingered a strand of her hair and his knuckles brushed her cheek. "I've got plans for you."

A shiver slid down her spine and her belly clenched with raw need. "What sort of plans?"

He leaned over and traced the shell of her ear with his tongue. Another hot shiver eddied through her and she felt her bones melt, her will—whatever remained of it—liquefy. "Depraved ones," he breathed.

She turned and caught his lips with her own, savoring the taste of him against her tongue. Her nipples pearled and her sex slickened and, for the moment, nothing mattered but him. He was her everything. Her very heart and illogically, she'd let him have it again.

"Ah," she whispered against his mouth. "Then I should probably just follow your lead."

He chuckled softly and the wicked sound melted over her heart like butter over a warm bun. "I like that plan best of all."

She rested her forehead against his and released a small sigh. A tangle of need and affection, regret and joy twisted her insides, making her breath catch. "I have a mortifying secret to confess."

His laugh was pure sin. "Yes?"

"That plan is rapidly becoming my favorite."

Following him had never been a problem—keeping up, on the other hand, was another matter altogether.

But tonight wasn't the night to think about that.

Tonight they were safely cocooned in this room and his depraved plans awaited

12

THE FIRST FINGERS OF dawn were crawling across the horizon when Tanner awoke the next morning, peeking through a small gap in the drapes. Something was different, he knew, but it took a couple of minutes to isolate the change.

No nightmare.

For the first time in four months, he hadn't dreamed of death and screaming, bloodied children or lifeless little bodies. He hadn't dreamed of the bombing, hadn't felt it rattle his teeth even though he knew it was impossible to truly feel something that was only happening in a nightmare.

Mia lay draped across his chest, her head resting over his heart, her leg slung over his thigh. Her small hand lay trustingly over his chest and he felt her hair trail over his arm, where he held her.

That was the difference, he realized.

She was the difference.

He'd been so consumed with obliterating every other

guy—any who'd come before or would come after—
from her mind and body that he'd worn himself out,
made himself too tired to even dream. He felt a slow
smile slide over his lips

And it had been heavenly.

The idea of leaving her today, of getting into the
car and going to the airport, of getting on a plane and
removing himself several hundred miles from her felt
wrong on more levels than he could count, but he knew it
was the only way. One nightmareless night didn't mean
that he was in any way ready to let her back into his life,
to let anyone in, for that matter. And he certainly didn't
want her to have to hold his hand through what he knew
would be countless setbacks.

Mia had said he was a good man, that he was not
weak, not a coward, and to some degree, he imagined
she was right. No one knew his failures and shortcom-
ings as well as he did, but he wasn't so blinded by his
immediate past anymore to forget that he had been a
good soldier, he had protected his country to the best of
his ability…for as long as he could. There was honor in
that and for the first time in months, he could see it.

But when it came to her…he was absolutely terrified
of failing her again, of not being the man she thought he
was. She'd known the idealistic boy determined to make
his mark, not the world-weary soldier who'd witnessed
senseless death and destruction. True, he'd been fighting
for the greater good, and he still believed in that, still
loved his country and respected the men who continued

to wear the uniform. On some level, he'd always be a soldier.

But he'd had the blinders ripped from his eyes and hadn't liked what he'd seen. It had been too much, too painful.

He simply couldn't get it out of his head—the images wouldn't leave him.

He was damaged goods now, disillusioned and jaded and, as much as he'd like to pretend that it had never happened, to just move forward and build a life with her, he didn't think he could and was too damned terrified to try. A bitter laugh built in the back of his throat.

In short, he was a coward, just a different variety.

He didn't want her to dust off that old dream again for him, not when the rubble from his own life would just muck it up.

She sighed sleepily against his chest and he knew the exact moment when she awoke. She flexed her toes and her eyelashes fluttered against his chest.

He rather liked that, Tanner thought.

"Rise and shine," he murmured, his voice rusty.

"How did you know I was awake?"

"Keen sense of intuition," he said.

"I moved, didn't I? Stretched."

"Actually, it was your eyelashes. They tickled me when you opened your eyes."

She hummed under her breath, a sleepy, happy sound. His chest squeezed. "You always wake up before I do."

"Habit," he murmured with effort. "Too many mornings getting up before dawn."

She laughed softly. "I am very rarely up before dawn." She peeked up at him. "You know what I noticed?"

"What?"

She smiled. "No nightmare last night."

"I know," he said, his throat strangely tight. "First time in four months. It was nice."

She propped up on one elbow. "Four months?" A line emerged between her brows. "You've been having those horrible dreams for four months?"

Tanner sighed. "Yes."

Concern tightened her eyes and she traced a finger along his chest. He watched her swallow. "Tanner, have you talked to someone? I don't mean me," she hastened to add. "I mean, a professional."

"I have," he admitted. "It's just going to take time. It has to get easier," he said.

"Because it can't get any worse? Has it gotten any better at all?"

"Since coming out of the military, you mean?"

She nodded.

"A little," he said, trying to lighten the moment. He gave her a squeeze. "I'd say last night was an improvement, a breakthrough even."

She rested her head against his chest once more, absently doodling her fingers over his belly. "Oh, Tanner," she said. "What am I going to do with you?" It was a rhetorical question, but he felt compelled to answer anyway.

"More of the same?" he suggested helpfully.

"You know what I mean." She paused. "I heard you,

you know," she said. "Not just the yelling," she clarified. "But you… You talked in your sleep."

He stilled and his heart rate kicked into overdrive. His mouth went bone-dry. "You heard me? What do you mean? What did I say?"

A beat slid to three. "I'm sorry," she told him. "I shouldn't have said anything."

Tanner chuckled grimly, dread balling in his gut. "That bad, eh?"

"You mentioned a school." She said it casually, as though it were just a minor little tidbit, but her tone didn't lessen the blow.

Tanner flinched.

She kissed his chest. "I'm so sorry."

Nausea clawed up his throat. "I'm sorry you had to hear that. I—"

She leaned up and glared at him. Her eyes were wet but fierce. "Don't you dare apologize to me for having to *hear* it," she scolded. "You *saw* it. You still can't get it out of your head. I can't even imagine… And I don't want to." She gave a delicate shudder. "It's too horrible to try. A school. It's unconscionable."

He chuckled grimly. "That's just it. The people who did it have no conscience. How do you fight something like that? The standard rules of war don't apply. We went in to help, to liberate the village—" bile rose in his throat, forcing him to swallow "—and they waited on a hill above the city until they saw us come in and remote detonated most of the town."

She gasped softly, seemingly horrified, then laid her head back on his chest. "Oh, Tanner."

"Bastards."

Her voice was hard when she spoke. "That's not a good enough epithet."

He silently concurred. "I was done after that, you know," he said. "I just…couldn't do it anymore." Bitterness crept into his tone. "And if it makes me weak, or cowardly or a disgrace to the Crawford name then so be it," he said. He stroked her hair. "I can live with that easier than I could the other."

"You are none of those things, Tanner Crawford, you hear me?" she said, giving him an emphatic squeeze. "None of them." Something wet and warm splashed against his chest. Her tears, he realized.

Startled, he raised her up. "Don't cry," he said, shushing her, wiping the moisture from the corner of her eye.

"It's just so sad," she said. "You hear things like this on the news, but we've grown so desensitized to it. It registers for a fleeting second, then it's gone and life goes on, you know. We're always a step removed."

"You're supposed to be. The military is the front line."

She shook her head. "I don't like that answer."

He kissed her salty cheek. "You wouldn't, would you, Bossy."

"I said it yesterday and I'm going to say it again because it bears repeating and, frankly, I think you need to hear it." She leaned up and looked him dead in the eye. "You're a good man, Tanner Crawford. You are *not* weak, you are *not* a coward and you damned sure aren't a disgrace." Her gaze softened and she reached up and traced her fingers along his cheek. There it was again, that affection. It slayed him. Left him breathless. "You have a noble heart, one that is good and true. And that's what I see when I look at you, not a coward. Never a coward." She framed his face with her hands and kissed him gently. "I'm so proud of you."

No one, not even his mother or grandfather, had ever said that to him before. A nebulous obstruction formed in his throat, preventing him from speaking. The person he'd wronged the most, the one he'd betrayed by leaving. *She* was proud of him. In that moment, her opinion became the only one that mattered. He merely nodded his thanks, then thanked her again the best way he knew how.

And he started with another kiss. And if this one was a bit desperate, then that's because he was.

BECAUSE SHE WAS DETERMINED not to let him see how much his confession upset her, the glib way he'd described what had happened to make him leave the military, Mia did all of her weeping in the shower. She wept for him, for the horrors he'd seen, for those poor children and their parents and, if she were honest, for herself, too.

Tanner Crawford was many things. He was funny, he was sexy, he was noble, loyal, fearless, honorable, brilliant and courageous, just to name a few.

He was also in no place to start a relationship.

She knew that. She'd known it going in. Right now Tanner was focused on being the best former soldier turned security expert that he could be. That meant keeping the clutter in his admittedly shattered life to a minimum.

She was clutter.

He didn't have to tell her that. She was all too familiar with his *modus operandi*—it was too much a part of who he was—and, whereas she'd briefly resented him for it all those years ago, in all honesty, she couldn't this time.

In just a few short hours they would arrive in Dallas and he would leave her again. And, once again, she'd pretend like it didn't matter.

But it did.

The thought of watching him walk out of her life once more, particularly in his current wounded state, was almost more than she could bear. But if he could bear what he currently carried, then she could do this for him. She could make it easy. What he was dealing with was hard enough. She wouldn't compound his difficulties by forming any expectations.

Mia had absolutely no regrets about being with Tanner again and she didn't want him to have any, either. In fact, the only regret she wanted to leave him with was the regret that they hadn't had more time together.

When she left the bathroom, her eyes were a little puffy, but they were dry.

He was on the phone. He stood at the desk and fiddled

with the desk pad, then idly flipped through the complimentary binder which outlined the motels amenities. They should add "Easy to monitor and exit if need be" to the list, Mia thought.

"I know, Gramps. Yeah," he said. "I think it's going to suit. It's different, but I'm working with some great guys. Former Rangers who had similar motivation for coming out," he trailed off, as though he'd said too much. He paused, stilled, and his gaze sharpened. "No, sir. You never told me that. I didn't know." He chuckled, shook his head. "Yes, sir, there are a lot things I imagine I don't know. I—" Another pause, presumably while his grandfather spoke. He ducked his head, evidently chastened. "Yes, sir. I shouldn't presume to know your mind. I should have called. I—" He listened once more and something in his gaze softened. "Fishing? Yeah, that'd be great. I'll get up there as soon as I can." He added a few assurances, then disconnected.

She didn't have to hear the other side of the conversation to know what had just happened. Tanner had evidently lumped his grandfather in with his father when it came to how the pair of them would react to his leaving. That assumption had apparently irritated the older man. Tanner clearly hadn't given him enough credit.

"I like your grandfather," Mia announced with a decisive nod.

He chuckled and his gaze swung to hers. "He's a good man. I was afraid he'd—" He hesitated.

"React in the same manner as your father?" Mia finished.

He nodded. "I never did anything well enough to suit Dad," Tanner told her, his voice only slightly bitter. "So his reaction to me leaving the military wasn't unexpected. I wasn't sure how my grandfather would feel about it, and to tell you the truth, I...just didn't want to know."

Because it would have been more terrible to be a disappointment to his grandfather than his father. She could understand that. From the sounds of things, his grandfather did, too.

"I had no idea you liked to fish," she said, changing the direction of the conversation to something lighter.

He grinned. "Gramps has a pond he stocks with catfish. When I was little, he'd take me down there and bait my hook with a bread ball. I caught an eighteen-pounder with a one of those when was I was ten." He chuckled, remembering, and passed a hand over his face.

"A bread ball? Seriously?" She'd never heard of that. Of course, she'd never been fishing so why would she have?

He nodded. "Nothing fancy for Gramps, not when something simple works just as well."

"Sounds like a smart man."

"He is," Tanner murmured, still lost in thought. His gaze landed on her feet and he grinned. "Back in the heels, I see," he said, his appreciative gaze drifting lazily from one end of her body to the other.

"Back to work today," she announced too brightly. "The heels are part of my uniform." They were red, a peep-toe pump with a gold heel. They'd been her promotion present to herself. She coordinated the rest of the outfit around them. Red skirt with a flutter hem, fitted jacket and a white silk cami.

"You look lovely," Tanner said, ducking his head in a reverent nod, looking adorably nervous about issuing the compliment.

Pleasure bloomed inside her already breaking heart. "Thank you."

He hesitated, looked longingly at her, his face a mixture of emotion she'd never seen on it before. Finally, he straightened. "We should go."

"I'm ready," she lied. "You've got Moe, right?"

He slapped the backpack slung over his shoulder. "He's right here."

"You still think he doesn't work?" she asked as they exited the room.

"I went hard the first time I saw you again and Moe was nowhere around," he said, to her astonishment. He put his fingers on the small of her back, propelling her forward. "He has absolutely no influence on my libido. You are one-hundred percent responsible for my behavior over the past few days, and if you try to tell me that Moe Dick is responsible for yours—that you were only attracted to me because of that little stone statue—I will have no choice but to pound the idea right out of your head. And that pounding will take place in bed," he added. "Which is only fitting, in my opinion."

It was the longest speech she'd ever heard him make. Her lips twitched. "I had no idea you felt so strongly about it."

He glared down at her. "You're laughing at me."

"No, I'm not," she said, smothering a damning chuckle. She flattened her lips. "I'm not. Really."

Tanner opened the car door for her, a sardonic smile on his unbelievably carnal mouth. "You're a piss-poor liar, you know that, Bossy?"

She hoped not, Mia thought. Because she was going to have to tell him a whopper when it came time to say goodbye.

EVERYTHING WAS IN PLACE, the man thought.

He was ready.

He was waiting.

He would win.

13

TANNER PULLED INTO the parking lot, as close to the back entrance as possible. Dread weighted his shoulders and a mass of it set in his belly, making him nauseous. Once Moe Dick was safely inside, his job was finished. He would return to Atlanta, having completed his first mission successfully for Ranger Security.

He should feel some sort of satisfaction right now, should be skating the edge of fulfillment. Instead, he felt strangely hollow inside. As though he were standing on the periphery of a huge canyon and the next step was going to see him hurled into a huge abyss of misery as yet unknown.

From the corner of his eye, he watched Mia swallow. She closed her eyes, took a deep breath, then opened them again.

She had her game face on.

She turned to him then, a smile on her lips. "We made it," she said, her voice not altogether steady.

He nodded, following her lead. "We did." He paused. "How much longer until you're home?" he asked.

"Two weeks."

"Would you mind if I called you sometime?" he asked, to his immense surprise. He'd planned a clean break, but he couldn't seem to make it. Couldn't summon the words that would separate her permanently from him again.

From the slightly astonished look on her face, he wasn't the only one surprised by his question. "Of course, not," she said. "You've got my number."

"And you've got mine."

She blinked. "I do?"

"Yes," he said. "I programmed it into your phone."

A slow smile slid over her lips. "Oh. Thank you."

Tanner hesitated, searched for the right words, the ones that would make her understand. "Look, Mia. I'm a mess right now, but I'm hoping that isn't always going to be the case. I—"

"I don't expect anything from you, Tanner," she interjected. "You and I...we're good. We're okay, you know? Call me," she told him. "Keep in touch this time. And if you ever need me, I can be there in...what? Four hours?" She smiled as if it didn't signify. "That's nothing, right?"

He chuckled softly. "Not after this trip, no," he said. He bent forward and kissed her, softly, lingeringly. "You're a special girl, Bossy."

She released an unsteady breath and smiled against his lips. "Let's go, Idiot."

He chuckled, grabbed the backpack, then walked around and opened Mia's door. He'd just gotten her suitcase out of the SUV when he heard a woman scream and a baby cry.

His stomach dropped. Sweat broke out over his shoulders and his hands started to shake.

Then he saw her, a woman at the foot of the back steps, a baby wrapped in a blanket in her arms. She appeared to have fallen down the stairs and the baby was wedged between herself and the pavement.

Oh, God.

He didn't think twice, never considered not helping. "Hold on," he told Mia, then darted forward to try and assist the woman. She was still screaming when he reached her and he dropped to his knees. *He could help* this *one,* Tanner thought. *He could save* this *child. It would be all right. He wouldn't fail this time.*

Then the woman looked up, tossed the baby out of the way, and aimed a gun at him.

Too late, he realized his mistake. God only knew what this one would cost him. The cry wasn't authentic and the blanket should have been a dead giveaway. Who wrapped their baby in a blanket in Texas in August?

He deserved to be shot for his own stupidity.

Someone, most definitely Ramirez, had done their homework.

"No!" Mia screamed. "Tanner!"

"Get up," the woman said under her breath. Despite the wig and heavy makeup, Tanner now recognized her. Ackerman's assistant—Alma Threadgill. Closer inspection revealed something else, too. He recognized her from a photo he'd looked at only yesterday, one that Payne had sent him of the women who'd come to visit Mia's father. She'd had very blond hair, cut short, and had changed her makeup, but it was definitely her. She'd used the name Marie Upton then. Who knew which was her real name? His lips twisted as he stared at the doll.

"It's a Cry Baby," she said. "Brilliant, eh? The perfect touch."

"Where's Ackerman?" Tanner asked her, trying to buy some time. He sized up Alma. He knew without a doubt she would shoot him if he gave her a reason, and so he shifted to the left, putting himself firmly in front of Mia.

"He's inside," she sneered. "Fool. He's fought me every step of the way, but we see who's won, don't we? Now hand me the backpack."

Did she really believe it was going to be that simple? Tanner wondered. He laughed softly, trying to decide the best way to unarm her. "Er…no."

Her face went comically blank. "What? What do you mean no?"

"Tanner, give her the damned backpack!" Mia shouted, seemingly equally terrified and exasperated. "The damned thing isn't worth dying over."

He was the one who was looking down the barrel of a gun, and she was still giving orders. Didn't she trust him at all? Didn't she know he'd been a *Ranger,* for God's sake? Tanner rubbed the bridge of his nose and summoned patience. "Babe, could you butt out? I'm not planning on dying. Not today, anyway."

Alma narrowed her eyes. "Just because you're not planning on it doesn't mean it can't be arranged."

"Who sent you?" Tanner asked her, shifting again to put himself between Alma and Mia, who damn her hide, had moved closer. What the hell was she doing?

Alma laughed derisively. "Like I'm going to tell you."

"You said you fooled Ackerman. That couldn't have been easy, pulling the wool over that wily old reporter's eyes. It was you who planted the GPS, wasn't it?" No doubt she got it from Charlie, but he couldn't risk the reaction from Mia, Tanner thought. Not this far into the game.

Predictably, playing to her vanity won. Nothing tripped up a criminal faster than their own perceived self-importance and Alma was no exception. She thought she'd been brilliant and was eager to share her own superiority.

"Of course, it was. I told him about it afterward and he was appalled, couldn't believe I'd been so sneaky. As if he's not sneaky. But I needed a cover and he was a good one. He's lonely." She shrugged. "It made him an easy mark."

"Why's he been so eager to investigate Moe Dick?"

"Who?"

"The statue," he clarified.

"He's convinced that your girl here—" she jerked her

head toward Mia "—has planted the rumors about the statue's powers herself, to generate more buzz for the exhibit."

"What?" Mia shrieked. "That's outrageous! I would never do such a dirty, underhanded thing!"

Alma looked past him to Mia. "That's exactly what your father said."

He heard Mia swear. "That bastard," she muttered.

Alma's gaze suddenly turned hard. "You hurt his feelings, you know. Refusing his phone calls. Like you're better than he is," she sneered.

Alma turned to glare at Tanner. "I've said too much. Give me the backpack or I'm going to shoot you."

He fully believed she would. If he made a grab for the gun, who knew where the shot would land? And her grip seemed surprising steady. She knew how to handle the weapon. He wasn't dealing with a novice here. That made things more delicate, but not impossible.

"You know how Texas is with the death penalty," Tanner continued, as though they were talking about the weather and not his life. "I know lethal injection is supposed to be a kinder, gentler form of capital punishment, but since the meds are dosed with a paralytic, it could actually be quite painful for you and no one would ever know. Since you wouldn't be able to scream."

She paled.

"Where's Charlie?" Tanner asked, edging closer to her. "He sent you alone to do his dirty work, did he?"

"He trusts me," she said, but he knew he'd struck a nerve by the tightening around her mouth. "And this isn't dirty work. This work is going to set us up for life. We're going to drink margaritas and lay on a Mexican beach, watch the waves roll in and out and never worry about money again."

"Ramirez is paying you that much, is he?"

"Whose Ramirez?" she quipped, clearly lying.

"Is that what you're supposed to say when they arrest you?"

"I'm not going to get arrested."

"What about Charlie?" he asked, firing the question at her before she could think. He moved closer still. Almost there... "You supposed to 'forget' his name, too? I hope you're getting well-paid for this, Alma, since you're the one who's taking all the risk here."

She frowned, seemingly agitated. "Just shut up and give me the backpack."

"He's not worth it," Mia told her. Her voice was closer, dammit. She'd moved. Why the hell didn't she stay behind the car door? "Trust me on this, Alma. I know."

The woman's fevered gaze swung to Mia once more. "You don't know anything!" she said bitterly. "All you had to do was talk to him. But you wouldn't because your whore of a mother poisoned your mind against him. That's what he said."

"My mother was not a whore," Mia said through her clenched jaw.

"Yes, she was and you are, too. You're a whore just like her. And you hurt his feelings," she repeated in a strange voice, one that made the hair on the back of

Tanner's neck rise. Alma's gaze darted between the two of them, then she smiled a terrible sort of smile, darted to the side and fired a shot at Mia.

Mia screamed.

Having read her body language and moved an instant before she got the round off, Tanner took the hit in the shoulder and staggered to his knees, struck numb with pain.

"Tanner!"

Alma jerked the backpack from his shoulder and took off. Tanner was on his feet in an instant and hurried after her, Mia right behind him. Something red whizzed past his head and tagged Alma in the back.

Mia's shoe.

Alma screamed as though she'd been shot and fell forward.

Tanner recovered the backpack and bent at the waist, trying to catch his breath. His shoulder burned as though he'd had a hot poker shoved into it and he could feel the blood getting sticky beneath his shirt. He quickly dialed 911 on his cell phone while he still could.

Mia caught up with him, her eyes wild with fear. "Oh, Tanner. Sit down, please. The police will be here in a minute."

"No," he said. "Let's get this inside." He had a job to do, dammit, and had taken a bullet for it.

He would complete his mission.

"What about her?" Mia asked. Alma still writhed on the ground, still laboring under the deluded impression that she'd been shot. No doubt the pointy heel of

Mia's shoe had felt like a bullet when it had nailed her in the back.

"I'm dying," Alma gasped. "Oh, God, you've gone and crippled me. I can't feel my legs. *I can't feel my legs!*"

Mia kicked her in the thigh, eliciting another cry of pain from the prostrate woman. "You felt that, didn't you, you stupid cow. Tell my father to rot in hell."

Mia held up her shoe and showed it to Tanner. "I told you they were practical. Idiot," she chided, glaring at him. "I can't believe you let that psychotic bitch shoot you."

"Better me than you," he said, shadows closing in on his vision.

The cops arrived and took Alma into custody. Mia wrapped her arm around his waist and helped him forward. He handed Moe Dick over to Ed once they got inside and, smiling, he lost consciousness.

"Tanner Crawford," the surgeon announced from the door. Mia popped up and hurried forward.

"I'm here for Tanner," she said.

"He came through with flying colors. It missed the bone, so no messy fragments to contend with. We extracted the bullet. He's going to need a bit of therapy, but otherwise we anticipate a full recovery."

Mia wilted with relief. "Good," she said, nodding. "Can I see him?"

"He'll be in recovery another hour, then we'll move him to a room. You can see him then."

Mia murmured her thanks and neglected to tell the good doctor that they'd have a hell of a time convincing Tanner to stay in the hospital overnight. They'd be lucky if he didn't check himself out the instant he regained consciousness. She was given the room number and told to wait there.

She did, quite miserably, until they rolled Tanner in sixty-nine minutes later.

"Don't make a fuss," he murmured thickly. "I'm fine."

She smoothed her trembling fingers over his forehead. "I know you're fine, fool. Who's being bossy now, eh?"

He laughed weakly.

"Do you need anything? Are you thirsty?"

"Ice chips," he said. "Can't have anything to drink yet."

Mia slipped a piece of ice from a nearby cup into his mouth. "Did they get Ramirez?" he asked.

"They did." She'd had a phone call from Ed while she waited for Tanner to come out of surgery. "And my father," she added, still angry over his part in this.

The only favor the man had actually ever done her was in leaving—he'd just been another mouth to feed when he'd lived with them—and she'd thought she was finished with him. He'd never cared about her, or her mother for that matter, but had always had an eye to the things he'd wanted. Unfortunately, he'd never wanted to pay for them.

Whether Ramirez had contacted her father or her

father had contacted Ramirez was never truly clear, but the pair of them were definitely working together. Mia's connection to the exhibit had been an opportunity her father couldn't resist. Charlie had paired Alma up with Ackerman to be his eyes and ears on the scene because he'd known Mia would have had him kicked out of the exhibit if she'd seen him. Between Ramirez's cash and her father's charm, finding Mia and following her had been easy. Ackerman had merely been a pawn.

The wily old reporter had already been around to check on Tanner and had apologized to Mia for first suspecting her of any wrongdoing and second, for any unwitting part he'd played in what had happened. The man had always been brash and abrasive. Seeing him cowed had been quite upsetting. She'd offered him an exclusive interview regarding Moe and promised to give him the full scoop on everything. It was possible that this could end up being the story that was going to make his career after all.

She relayed all of this to Tanner, who alternated between extreme periods of alertness to drooping lids brought on by the medication. She had one more thing to tell him and hoped like hell he wouldn't be angry with her.

"I alerted Brian Payne at Ranger Security," she said.

Tanner's eyes widened. "Mia," he said, her name an accusation.

"Don't be mad," she said, giving his hand a squeeze. She loved his hands, so masculine, so competent, so wonderful against her skin. "They needed to know." She winced. "And I also called your mother."

He swore hotly, a word she hadn't ever heard him use. "You didn't," he said fully alert now. "You couldn't have done that to me. She'll hover. She'll fret." He said those things as if they were torture devices. "I'll *hate* it."

Mia straightened and glared at him. "Too damned bad," she said. "Be glad you've still got a mother who will hover and fret over you. You were *shot*, Tanner," she told him, as though explaining this to a two-year-old. "You can't get shot and not tell your mother." She threaded her fingers through his. "She's on her way and will be flying home with you."

Tanner studied her for a moment, his gaze searching hers. For what, who knew? But she could feel the change all the same. "I could cheerfully throttle you."

She sighed, then smiled. "But you won't, because you know I'm right."

"Since you've managed everything else, I'm assuming that you've talked to my surgeon. When am I getting out of here?"

"Tomorrow afternoon, provided you don't develop a fever."

"I won't," he said.

Mia merely laughed.

His gaze slid over her again, lingering on her mouth. "When do you have to be back?"

"It doesn't matter," she said. "I'm not leaving until your mother gets here." And she wasn't. She couldn't leave him alone. She didn't know how all of this was ultimately going to affect him. Hearing Alma scream, the fake baby cry. All that was missing was a damned bomb. Damned Ramirez. He'd certainly done his homework, had known exactly what buttons to push. She'd watched every bit of the color leech out of Tanner's face when he'd seen the stage Alma had set. And to top it off, he'd been shot. Because he'd been protecting her. She'd been Alma's target and Tanner had put himself between her and a bullet.

And his father had the audacity to say this man was a coward. Bullshit. He was a hero—*her hero*—and he'd forever own her heart.

She'd literally felt her heart stop when she'd seen him leap in front of that gun. She'd thought he was dead, that Alma had killed him…and she'd been powerless to stop it.

It was the single most horrible moment in her life and it was nothing—*nothing*—compared to what he'd witnessed. It sort of put things into perspective for her.

Tanner squeezed her hand. "Mia, you don't have to stay. You'll need your rest. The exhibit opens tomorrow."

"And I'll be there," she said. "But for now, I'm here with you. Budge up, would you?" she said, crawling into bed with him. She rested her head against his good shoulder. "You scared the hell out of me, you know that? No more jumping in front of bullets meant for other people," she told him. "Even me. My nerves can't handle it."

He laughed sleepily. "I couldn't let her hurt you.

You're my Bossy." She swallowed hard, dashed a tear off her cheek.

And then his breathing leveled off and he slept. When his mother arrived at seven, he was still asleep.

The bad news? She was leaving him again.

The good news? No nightmares.

Extracting a promise from his mother to let her know how Tanner was doing, Mia pressed a kiss to his temple, breathed him in for a moment, and left.

Strangely, it was even harder this time.

14

Two weeks later...

LEAVING ENOUGH HOMEMADE FOOD in the fridge to last him for the rest of the year, Tanner's mother kissed him on the cheek and abruptly took her leave. She'd been with him for the past two weeks, from the flight home right up until now, when she'd suddenly announced that it was time for her to go back to Aunt Margaret's. She had to pick flooring and look at paint swatches for the new house. She had places to go, people to see, things to do.

Interestingly, he'd been asking her when she planned to go home almost every day since they'd gotten back from Dallas and every day he'd gotten the same vague answer, even as early as this morning. She'd taken a call, presumably from his sister, a couple of hours ago and had made quick work of putting the finishing touches on the chicken casserole she'd left on the stove to cool. Then she packed her bag for her immediate departure.

Bizarre.

She'd been gone all of two minutes when his doorbell rang again. She must have forgotten something, Tanner thought, as he made his way to the door. Though he'd been out of the house for more than a dozen years, he had to admit that having his mom here had been unexpectedly nice. She'd doted on him and her hovering had actually been a pleasant distraction from the fact that he was well and truly miserable without Mia.

He'd been miserable before, of course, but it was a damned sight more noticeable now.

Simply put…he missed her.

He'd called her a couple of times since getting home and just hearing her voice had made something ache inside him. Unfortunately, though she always sounded happy to hear from him, she didn't seem to be suffering from the same heartsickness he'd been stricken with. She always sounded busy. She was making time to talk to him, sure, but he got the impression that, were she not talking to him, she'd have something else to do. Some other pressing matter. Her work, he imagined.

Meanwhile, he'd been put out of commission for another two weeks. Damned gunshot wound. He'd managed to do half a dozen tours of duty without getting himself shot, but his first assignment for Ranger Security, he ended up taking metal. It was unbelievable.

Jamie had noted the opened condom box when he'd come over to do an upgrade on his computer and had simply raised an eyebrow in response. What could Tanner say? His lips twisted with humor. Somehow "thank you" didn't seem appropriate.

He opened the door and shock glued his tongue to the roof of his mouth.

Mia.

"Hi," she said, almost shyly. "I hope you don't mind that I showed up without asking first."

He gave his head a shake. "No, of course, not. Come in," he said, stepping back to allow her into the apartment. He gave her a hug, inhaling the scent of peaches, and pressed a kiss to her lips. He could have lingered forever, but didn't. Instead, he showed her down the hall to the living room. "Can I get you something to drink? Coffee? Beer? Whiskey?"

"No," she said, sitting on the edge of his couch. She looked around, inspecting his place. "This is nice," she said. "The perfect bachelor pad, eh?"

"The technology is nice," he admitted. "But my taste runs to natural woods and antiques."

She blinked, seemingly surprised. "Really?"

"Yeah," he said, delighted that he'd shocked her. It was nice to put that shoe on the other foot for a change.

"You would have liked my place then. A Craftsman. I just put it on the market." She said it casually, but his antennae twitched all the same.

"You're selling your house? You're moving?"

She turned to look at him, fidgeted uncertainly. It was so out of character of her that he started to get nervous. Was something wrong? Had she been transferred? Was she going to study the mating habits of the some unknown culture in Africa? The idea punched his heart rate into the panic zone.

He couldn't let her leave, couldn't let her go. Four hours was too far already. He'd been going crazy for the past two weeks. He'd come to the decision that if she could stand him for four days the way he'd been, then he wasn't giving her enough credit. She could obviously stand him for a longer period of time.

Like forever.

"I am moving, actually. To Atlanta."

"What?" Joy bolted through him.

"I'm transferring to The High Museum."

He felt his grin broaden. "You are? That's wonderful. Was this a request or a mandate?" Dare he hope she wanted to be closer to him? That she wanted to give this a go between them?

"It was a request, actually," she admitted. She studied the volumes on his coffee table, smiling when she saw the book of Poe he'd added. He was wearing the hell out of eBay. He'd also been looking for something else, but hadn't found it yet. "You see...I wanted my baby to be closer to its father."

Sound receded for a minute. "Your baby," he repeated. "Its father."

His gaze tangled with hers and she gave a little laugh. She rubbed her hand over her still flat belly. "Proof positive Moe works," she said. Her voice was unnaturally high and woefully uncertain.

It took him much longer than it should to connect the

dots, but when he did, his eyes widened and he smiled wonderingly. "You're pregnant?"

"I am. Quite happily, by the way." She watched him cautiously, still waiting for his reaction. "I know that you—"

He dropped to his knees and knelt between her legs, placed his hand over hers. His eyes burned. "I'm going to be a father," he interrupted, still stunned, knocked stupid with happiness.

"You are," she confirmed, laughing softly, seemingly surprised at his response. "Are you okay with this, Tanner? I've been taking a shot every three months for years. My birth control shouldn't have failed, but—"

"But your birth control was no match for my virility," he said, practically chortling with glee. He suddenly wanted to beat his chest and roar. "You're pregnant," he said again. "*We're* pregnant. We're going to have a baby."

He peered at her belly as though he could see through her abdomen to the little life nestled safely inside.

"So you're happy?" she asked.

He looked up at her. "You know the answer to that already. Nobody knows me better than you, Mia. No one ever has." He kissed her fingers. "I love you, Bossy. You ought to know that, as well."

Her eyes welled with tears and a watery smile shaped her lips. "I think you should propose to me now."

He laughed and shook his head. "I was getting to that part," he said. "You pre-empted me."

"That's because I'm always one step ahead of you."

He sighed. "I had a plan," he said.

She inclined her head. "Does it involve me following your lead?"

"It does."

Mia looped her arms around his neck and kissed him. "Good," she murmured. "Because that one, as you know, is my all-time favorite."

Epilogue

Two weeks later...

"THEY LOVE YOU, YOU KNOW," Tanner told her.

Mia looked around at her new family and felt more at peace, accepted and content than she ever had in her life. She and Tanner had traveled to Asheville and had married there, in his sister's backyard. Roxy lived in an old antebellum house, with a beautiful courtyard in the back. It was the perfect place for tossing a football or hosting a wedding, one that her new sister-in-law had organized with amazing rapidity without sacrificing class.

Mia wore her mother's dress—she'd been saving it— and Tanner's grandfather had offered to give her away. She'd been more touched by that than anything else. Tanner's father was absent and sadly, Mia didn't think that the relationship would ever be repaired, but some relationships were like that, she thought. Better left to die a natural death than to try and hold on to something that was toxic.

Their baby would have a doting grandmother and great-grandfather and a host of aunts and uncles—some related and some not—to help round out his or her family. It would be loved and that was all that mattered.

All three founders of Ranger Security had made the drive for the occasion, two of them bringing their wives. Mia had taken an instant liking to Payne's wife, Emma, and Guy McCann's other half was sure to be a fast friend, as well. Mia looked forward to meeting Jamie's wife, Audrey, who was in Maine at the moment. Jamie had intended to go up and see her this weekend, but had come to their wedding instead. That gesture spoke volumes about how these men regarded her new husband and she was eternally grateful for that regard.

Mia smiled up at Tanner and pressed a kiss against his lips, licking a bit of cake from the corner of his mouth in the process.

"Unless you want to start the honeymoon in front of everyone, you'd better quit that right now."

"I don't want to start the honeymoon in front of everyone, but I am ready to start it right this very second," she said. She looped her arms around his neck. "I'm *extraordinarily* ready," she said significantly.

Tanner chuckled low, her favorite sound. "Are we dealing with pregnancy hormones already? I've heard about those."

"I don't think so," she told him. "You just make me hot. You always have. You're the only one who's ever done it for me, you know. The only one who has ever rung my bell, so to speak."

He drew back and looked down at her. "*I'm* the only one? But I thought you said—"

She winced. "I might have told a little fib or two regarding—"

Tanner's smile was laced with pure masculine satisfaction. "You lied," he said, seemingly impressed with her duplicity.

"And you said I wasn't good at it," she reminded him, preening a bit. "Fooled you, didn't I?"

"So I'm the only one who has ever made you—"

"Yes," she confirmed. "Only ever you. Now spit the canary out of your mouth," she said, referred to his smile. "Those feathers don't match your tux."

"I hope you didn't waste money on a wedding gift," Tanner told her, all but rocking back on his heels. "Because as far as I'm concerned that was it."

"It'll just have to be a bonus then," Mia said. "Because I've already got your gift. It's packed in my luggage. I was going to give it to you tonight, but I'd like to tell you what it is."

"Is it a nightie?" he asked hopefully. "Something see-through?"

She chuckled. "I've got one of those, too, but that's not your wedding gift, either."

"Damn," he said. "This feels like Christmas. Go on, then. Tell me," he said indulgently.

"I've got two tickets to Baltimore for January 19th."

His eyes crinkled at the corners. "To see the Poe Toaster?"

She nodded. "If anyone carries on the tradition, we're going to be there for it. Just don't let me freeze to death."

"Don't worry," he said. "I can think of several ways to keep you warm."

Of that, she had no doubt.

"I've got something for you, too," Tanner told her. "And it's not in my luggage. It's in my pocket."

Her heart-rate kicked up a notch. "Are you going to let me have it."

He withdrew a small velvet box and handed it to her. Hands shaking, Mia opened it and gasped.

Her great-grandmother's ring, the one that had belonged to her mother. Tears filled her eyes. "Tanner," she said, for lack of anything better.

"It's a replica," he said. "I took the photo to a jeweler and had him make it for you. I know it's not the real thing, but I wanted you to have it anyway. We'll keep looking for the original, but in the meantime..." He stopped, as though suddenly uncertain of his gift.

She slid it onto her finger and watched the opal, diamonds and rubies catch the light, then she looked up at him. "Thank you," she said thickly. "It's perfect.

Absolutely perfect. You couldn't have given me anything I would have loved more."

He nodded, seemingly relieved. His gaze searched hers. "I'm the one making out like a bandit here," he said. "I got you."

And *she'd* gotten *him*.

Finally.

* * * * *

COMING NEXT MONTH

Available August 31, 2010

REQUEST YOUR FREE BOOKS!

2 FREE NOVELS PLUS 2 FREE GIFTS!

HARLEQUIN®

Blaze

Red-hot reads!

YES! Please send me 2 FREE Harlequin® Blaze™ novels and my 2 FREE gifts (gifts are worth about $10). After receiving them, if I don't wish to receive any more books, I can return the shipping statement marked "cancel." If I don't cancel, I will receive 6 brand-new novels every month and be billed just $4.24 per book in the U.S. or $4.71 per book in Canada. That's a saving of at least 15% off the cover price. It's quite a bargain. Shipping and handling is just 50¢ per book.* I understand that accepting the 2 free books and gifts places me under no obligation to buy anything. I can always return a shipment and cancel at any time. Even if I never buy another book, the two free books and gifts are mine to keep forever.

151/351 HDN E5LS

Name	(PLEASE PRINT)
Address	Apt. #
City	State/Prov.	Zip/Postal Code

Signature (if under 18, a parent or guardian must sign)

Mail to the **Harlequin Reader Service:**
IN U.S.A.: P.O. Box 1867, Buffalo, NY 14240-1867
IN CANADA: P.O. Box 609, Fort Erie, Ontario L2A 5X3

Not valid for current subscribers to Harlequin Blaze books.

Want to try two free books from another line?
Call 1-800-873-8635 or visit www.morefreebooks.com.

* Terms and prices subject to change without notice. Prices do not include applicable taxes. N.Y. residents add applicable sales tax. Canadian residents will be charged applicable provincial taxes and GST. Offer not valid in Quebec. This offer is limited to one order per household. All orders subject to approval. Credit or debit balances in a customer's account(s) may be offset by any other outstanding balance owed by or to the customer. Please allow 4 to 6 weeks for delivery. Offer available while quantities last.

Your Privacy: Harlequin Books is committed to protecting your privacy. Our Privacy Policy is available online at www.eHarlequin.com or upon request from the Reader Service. From time to time we make our lists of customers available to reputable third parties who may have a product or service of interest to you. If you would prefer we not share your name and address, please check here. ☐
Help us get it right—We strive for accurate, respectful and relevant communications. To clarify or modify your communication preferences, visit us at www.ReaderService.com/consumerchoice.

HB10

HARLEQUIN®

A Romance

FOR EVERY MOOD™

Spotlight on
Heart & Home

Heartwarming romances
where love can happen
right when you least expect it.

See the next page to enjoy a sneak peek
from Harlequin Superromance®,
a Heart and Home series.

Enjoy a sneak peek at fan favorite Molly O'Keefe's
Harlequin Superromance miniseries,
THE NOTORIOUS O'NEILLS, *with*
TYLER O'NEILL'S REDEMPTION,
available September 2010
only from Harlequin Superromance.

Police chief Juliette Tremblant recognized the shape of the man strolling down the street—in as calm and leisurely fashion as if it were the middle of the day rather than midnight. She slowed her car, convinced her eyes were playing tricks on her. It had been a long time since Tyler O'Neill had been seen in this town.

As she pulled to a stop at the curb, he turned toward her and her heart about stopped.

"What the hell are you doing here, Tyler?"

"Well, if it isn't Juliette Tremblant." He made his way over to her, then leaned down so he could look her in the eye. He was close enough to touch.

Juliette was not, repeat, *not* going to touch Tyler O'Neill. Not with her fingers. Not with a ten-foot pole. There would be no touching. Which was too bad, since it was the only way she was ever going to convince herself the man standing in front of her—as rumpled and heart-stoppingly handsome now as he'd been at sixteen—was real.

And not a figment of all her furious revenge dreams.

"What are you doing back in Bonne Terre?" she asked.

"The manor is sitting empty," Tyler said and shrugged as though his arriving out of the blue after ten years was casual. "Seems like someone should be watching over the family home."

"You?" She laughed at the very notion of him being here for any unselfish reason. "Please."

He stared at her for a second, then smiled. Her heart fluttered against her chest—a small mechanical bird powered by that smile.

"You're right." But that cryptic comment was all he offered.

Juliette bit her lip against the other questions.

Why did you go?

Why didn't you write? Call?

What did I do?

But what would be the point? Ten years of silence were all the answer she really needed.

She had sworn off feeling anything for this man long ago. Yet one look at him and all the old hurt and rage resurfaced as though they'd been waiting for the chance. That made her mad.

She put the car in gear, determined not to waste another minute thinking about Tyler O'Neill. "Have a good night, Tyler," she said, liking all the cool "go screw yourself" she managed to fit into those words.

It seems Juliette has an old score to settle with Tyler.
Pick up TYLER O'NEILL'S REDEMPTION
to see how he makes it up to her.
Available September 2010,
only from Harlequin Superromance.